# Dust of Lies

# Dust of Lies

## G.K. Davenport

 Fiction
Edmond, Oklahoma

4RV Publishing
2912 Rankin Terrace, Edmond, OK 73083
http://4rvpublishing.com

cover art copyright © 2020 by Steve Daniels and 4RV Publishing
book design by Elizabeth Morgan and Aidana WillowRaven

Library of Congress TXu 1-994-014

ISBN-13 paperback: 978-1-950074-07-5
ISBN-13 hardcover: 978-1-950074-08-2

 Fiction
Printed in the United States of America

# Dedication

I dedicate this book to my precious daughter, Kimberly Marie Botts (1971-2014). She was, and shall always be, the axis of my world.

# *Dust of Lies*

*Changing winds scoured the face of the prairie.*
*Sands of truth blasted blue-grey skies.*
*The tempest ceased; the land grew quiet.*
*All lay shrouded in the Dust of Lies.*

# Chapter I

I stood in the blistering heat, my nose torched red by the blazing sun. The air hung heavy with stifling humidity. Rivulets of perspiration trickled down my cheeks and the back of my neck, collecting in a sweat-slick between my shoulders. But, nothing could keep me from witnessing Skeeter's old bulldozer crush the tar out of the abandoned county jail, not even the burning assault of a sultry Arkansas afternoon.

As the only reporter for the *Barber Gazette*, I felt a duty to record the demolition of one of the few remaining relics of a bygone era. I needed to take a few pictures, write my column, and give Thursday's weekly paper a headline to commemorate its historic passing.

A small band of locals milled around as Skeeter aligned his ancient machine head-on with the crumbling edifice. He revved the engine twice, sending soot clouds billowing out of the exhaust and, with great deliberation, inched the lumbering dozer toward its target. The blade grabbed the base of the rickety structure, lifting the stucco and timber off its foundation. The jail resisted the onslaught with the stamina of a primal warrior. Again and again, Skeeter retreated and took aim. Gears groaned as the iron beast waged battle against walls of ancient brick and mortar, sending rotten timbers crashing to the ground in a tangled mass of metal roofing. Broken slabs of plaster teetered on heaps of debris, encased in a powdery fog of dust. Slowly, the dust settled, signaling the end of the primitive house of incarceration.

The sun had passed its prime, sinking low in the west. The fiery ball now rested on the shoulders of Sugar Loaf Mountain, allowing evening shadows to stalk the little valley town of Barber. I panicked. The demolition consumed most of the afternoon, and I still had work to do. I snapped pictures and interviewed a few spectators. As I turned to leave, a string of words scrawled on a busted block of plaster caught my eye. The broken block reminded me of a weathered grave marker, like the ones found in long-forgotten cemeteries. Bending, I traced the letters with my finger, revealing the words of a poem:

> Here I hang
> With my face to the wall
> Ora Price was the cause
> Of it all!

I stopped and stared at the poem; the words resonating in my head. *What happened here?*

I knew very little of the community lore. I moved to Barber a few years ago so my husband could care for his elderly mother. This job with the newspaper helped me hold on to my sanity. To my surprise, I enjoyed getting to know the community, although, I covered fairly unsensational stories. This poem, however, intrigued me. *Who wrote it? Who was Ora Price?* Local lore or not, I could bet my last dollar that the story surrounding this poem would surpass any article I normally publish — and I intended to get to the bottom of it.

Skeeter lived in Barber all his life. If anyone could tell me about the poem's history, he could. This man looked almost as old as the jail he tore down. Skeeter backed up his trailer to a dirt ledge and prepared to load the dozer. The deafening roar of the engine prompted me to flail my hands to flag him down. He turned the engine off and sauntered in my direction in soot-soiled overalls. As he reached the sidewalk bordering the rubble, he stopped to survey his work. A grin spread across his craggy face, exposing uneven, discolored teeth.

"What does this mean?" I asked, pointing to the slab.

Skeeter's face tightened, his lips narrowing to pencil-thin lines. "I don't know nothin' about that, miss. Now, if you'll excuse me, I will go on about my business." His tone booked no reply.

*Wow! What a strong response to a simple question. Or was it simple?*

More curious than ever, I took off toward my mother-in-law's house. Viva lived four miles outside of Barber at the base of Sugar Loaf Mountain. Tall pines and poplars circled the simple, two-story farmhouse, protecting it from the invasion of change. Built in 1898, its age showed. Flat, sandstone boulders provided the foundation for the tall, clapboard structure flanked by two screened-in porches, one in front and one in back. By the time I pulled up to her house, dusk had settled in the shadows of the towering mountain. The lateness of the hour concerned me, but not enough to derail my mission.

Of the seventy-nine years of her life, Viva spent the last seventy years here. Small towns are not leakproof. If the poem had any significance, she would have some clues.

I tapped on Viva's door as I turned the knob to let myself in. She sat, as usual, in her recliner with the TV blaring. She hadn't heard me enter. Although her hearing had diminished with time, her mind remained intact. If she ever knew anything about the poem, she would remember.

"I hope I am not intruding," I called.

An elongated mirror at the end of the foyer halted my advance. It captured my five-foot, four frame from head to toe. A ragged waif stole my identity. Wisps of reddish-brown hair escaped the clasp securing my ponytail and lay plastered on my cheeks and neck. A sweat-dampened tee-shirt clung to my scrawny frame. Smudged eyeliner rimmed my eyes. My brown eyes looked as if they had melted and spilled over the brims. I rubbed at the smudges of makeup before pushing the tendrils of hair back in place. *It will have to do*, I thought, as I strolled over to give Viva a hug.

She returned my hug politely but with a slight air of indifference. We did not have a warm relationship. I hesitated to continue, but I could not stem my deep curiosity about the poem.

"Have a seat, Kay. You know you are always welcome."

"I need your help with an article I'm writing." I pulled the small rocker from the corner of the room and sat as close as possible to her chair. Yes, I stretched the truth, but I needed to broach the topic of the poem. Taking a deep breath, I went on.

"I watched the demolition of the old jail today. I saw this poem written on a slab in the rubble. It said, "'Here I hang …'"

Viva picked up the recitation. "With my face to the wall, Ora Price was the cause of it all."

"That's it! Do you know Ora? Do you know who wrote this poem?"

Recognition lit the watery, blue eyes faded with age.

"Yes," she said. "I knew Ora."

Her drawl made the word "yes" sound more like "yay us." She redirected her eyes to the TV.

"And?" I prodded.

"And, what, dear?"

"What do you know about Ora and the poem?" I asked, controlling the impatience in my voice. "Why would Ora Price be the cause of a man hanging himself?"

She clicked the off button on the remote control and turned to face me. She studied my face for a few moments as if to determine what I really wanted to know.

My relationship with her floundered from day one. We interacted like strangers bound together by my husband. I married her only son two years ago, my first marriage and his second. The death of Darrell's first wife, Kendra, devastated Viva. I watched her face as she studied mine, looking for signs of her disapproval of me.

A self-professed nerd and a studious introvert who devoted most of her life to teaching science at the University of Arkansas, I hid behind books, research, and projects all my life. Although I could almost call them my family, sometimes I felt as if I viewed life through a window with my nose pressed against the glass, seeing but not touching the lives of the people around me. I wanted to be on the other side of the windowpane. When I married Darrell, I chose to relinquish the burden of ambition and replace it with a real life. Would Viva ever approve of his choice?

After a long, unrelenting silence, she rose slowly from her chair, allowing her arthritic bones to adjust to her weight before shuffling down the hall toward her bedroom. I waited in silence, wondering why on earth she left without any explanation. She returned with a tattered shoebox under her arm. She sat down again and placed the box on the coffee table. She sorted carefully through a collection of yellowed papers, rendered fragile by the passing of time, until she found what she was looking for.

"Read this, Kay."

### "EZRA HACKER SELF-EXECUTED"

Ezra Hacker, son of the Rev. A.C. Hacker, hanged himself in jail here last Saturday night.

He had been jailed for several days on a charge of wife abandonment and Saturday told his father he would kill himself if he did not get out. He thought he was joking.

Hacker cut the ropes from the window weights, and tied one end to the top of the sill and the other around his neck, and drew his feet up from the floor.

He was dead when jailor Caps went to feed him Sunday morning. Justice Castleberry summoned a jury and held an inquest which, after viewing the body, rendered a verdict to the effect he died by his own hands.

In the upper-right corner, someone scribbled the date: 12-19-1919.

"A man hung himself with a window weight over wife abandonment. What has this got to do with the poem about Ora?" I said.

Her eyes widened. "Ezra Hacker was only nineteen when he hanged himself. He and Ora married when she was fifteen, and he was eighteen. They had a baby boy named Joseph, who was born in November ... just a few weeks before the hanging."

Excitement stirred inside me. Viva knew the story.

"I met Ora about that time," she said. "We'd just moved to Barber so Papa could begin his ministry with the church. Ezra Hacker's funeral was the first he ever preached. I remember it like it happened yesterday. Ora came with her stepdad, Ben Townsend, and her mother, Ellie, to make the funeral arrangements." Viva shook her head. "What a pitiful slip of a girl. She hung in her mother's shadow, just like her mother hung in Ben's shadow. But, Ben, that's another story. Blustery, self-righteous — and forgive me for saying so — a pompous ass."

I had never heard her use vulgarity. My interest perked up.

"He *strutted* into Papa's office at the church like he owned the place." Viva swung her bent arms from side to side and marched in place, mimicking Ben. "I could hear him hollering, saying he didn't think Ezra deserved a Christian burial because he committed suicide. I watched through a keyhole, you understand, but I could see it all. Ben raised Papa's dander. Ora stood there, frozen, and stared at the wooden floor. Her mother kept talking, kept pleading with Ben. After a while, his rantings stopped. Papa and Ellie made funeral arrangements, while Ben sat in stony silence. Ora just stared."

Viva glanced at me, measuring my reaction.

"That was the first time I came across Ora and her family, but not my last," she murmured as she leaned her head back and closed her eyes.

I wanted to hear more, but she appeared to have fallen asleep. Her jaw slackened, and her pleated eyelids closed. I still had no inkling how Ora "was the cause of it all," but it looked like I would not find out today. As I rose, Viva clenched my arm with a surprisingly strong grip. She was awake.

"Kay, there's more to this than anyone would ever suspect," she said in a warning tone. "I've kept Ora's story to myself for so many years … maybe this is a sign, you showing up like this. Maybe it's time for the truth to come out. Promise me you won't let it die or let the others influence you. You've started this. Please finish it."

"Of course." I had no idea what I started or what I would need to finish. *And, who on earth were the "others?"*

# Chapter II

I made a quick trip to the local courthouse the next morning, hoping to find out more about Ezra and his suicide, but this small Barber town lacked records of any consequence. Booneville proved little better. I revisited Viva, hoping she would be up to more stories.

I got lucky. Viva seemed to have a rekindled interest in Ora, and I appeared to be her newfound audience. She needed little to no encouragement to pick up from where she left off yesterday.

"Ora was so much like her mother," Viva said, settling back more comfortably into her chair, "and she seemed to be going through what her mother did. Ellie's first husband was Samuel Price. They had two girls. Pneumonia took him when the girls were little. She married Ben Townsend after Samuel's passing."

"That must have been difficult for her." I envisioned a woman with two small children, afraid throughout her husband's illness and panicked after he died.

"Not much else for a widow to do in those years than remarry," said Viva matter-of-factly. "If memory serves me right, Ben's first wife was named Cornelia." She tapped a finger to her cheek as she reflected. "Uh-huh. Rachel Cornelia Hooper. I think she and Ben had six children."

*Wow!* *Two young girls of her own and six stepchildren.* The image unsettled me.

Viva seemed immersed in the past, oblivious to my presence. She closed her eyes as if better to remember. "When Ellie married Ben, she wasn't that much older than his oldest child, poor lamb. And, you can bet they gave her a hard time. Ben was no better. He was downright mean to her. He told her he'd give up all of 'em to have his Cornelia." She harrumphed. "Fancy that. Telling his new wife he would throw all of 'em away just to get his first wife back."

Many women struggle with the ghost of a first wife. It would crush me if Darrell ever said that about Kendra.

Viva opened her eyes and peered at me. "I wish I could judge him a little more kindly, but I can't," she said. "You know how I lost my husband? In a freak accident on the Mississippi River back in '59. Broke my heart, but I had to move on. You don't forget someone you love. You don't love them any less, but most people find room in their heart to love someone again. Life goes on." She paused. "I think I was right about Ben, though. There really wasn't room in his heart to love anyone but Cornelia."

As we sat in silence, collecting our thoughts, I wondered if Viva meant for her words to serve as a message to me. *If life went on, why are Kendra's pictures still on the mantelpiece?*

"I didn't mean to go off on that subject," she blurted. "What I'm trying to say is that Ben was old, probably not thinking right and maybe just talking. But, that's no excuse to be so mean and hateful." She shifted restlessly. She had been sitting for too long. I extended my hand to help her out of the chair, but she brushed it aside and struggled to her feet alone. Did she need her independence? Or would the touch of my hand threaten the ethereal bond she shared with Kendra?

Viva tottered into the bathroom. A few minutes later, I heard the toilet flushing, and then she shuffled back into the living room and eased into her chair. "Now, where were we?" she asked. "Oh, yes, we were talking about Ben and Ellie."

I nodded. "So, what happened to them?"

"Well," she said, "they married for convenience, really quite common back in those days. Ben was like a lot of men. He expected to be lord of the house and waited on. Ellie's work never ended." She hesitated, and I thought I might see tears pricking the corners of her eyes. "She died at fifty-two. She went out to milk the cow in the barn … just didn't come in. When they checked on her, she was dead."

*How awful.* I did not know what to say.

"Oddly enough, Ora showed me the report attached to the death certificate. She vomited bloody stuff all that morning, don't you know, sicker than a dog. I've often wondered why, when there were at least two able-bodied men in the house, *they* weren't out milking."

Indignation rang in Viva's words. She stopped talking and leaned back in her chair. Even though she meandered a little, I did not want to interrupt Viva's account of Ellie's life. In the few years I'd known her, we never had a truly personal conversation. Ora's story opened the dam and allowed all of her words to come flooding out.

"They didn't even know each other when they got married. Can you picture that?" said Viva. "After Cornelia died, Ben needed a woman to raise his six children. Pure and simple. He went to the local drugstore where men with time on their hands played checkers and drank coffee. Ben told them he needed a wife. Someone mentioned this young widow with two small girls. Maybe she wanted a man. Ben climbed in his buckboard and rode the seven miles to the Price place with one goal in mind — to get a wife."

"Apparently, he did," I commented.

"He sure did." A grimace tugged at the corners of her mouth. "She needed a husband to provide for her children and didn't have a lot of choices. Ellie was sitting on the front porch of the old farmhouse when he drove up. Ben told her he needed a woman to run his household. He said the crops were ready to harvest from the fields, and that he would return when he finished gathering the wheat. If she wanted to marry, she must have her bags packed and be ready to go. What kind of proposal is that?"

Viva stopped talking and looked at me. "Can you imagine?"

I truly couldn't, and I feared interrupting her story.

"So, what happened then?" I asked.

"Well, he came back just like he said. Ellie was shelling peas on the front porch when he arrived. Ben looked at her and said, 'Well?' Without a word, Ellie wrapped the shelled peas in the apron she was wearing, packed the peas and the few clothes she and the girls owned in a trunk and loaded them in the wagon. They headed straight for the minister's house and got hitched without getting off the buckboard."

"Poor Ellie."

Viva widened her eyes and sat up straight. "Poor Ellie's children. Ben Townsend was a cold, Bible-thumping fool who felt little for anyone after Cornelia. Ora couldn't wait to leave. I think that was why she married Ezra so young."

"But, she went from one angry man to another."

"Did she?" Viva smirked like she knew something I didn't. "Your poem, there — I think the person you need to find out about is Cowboy."

She made the word sound like a proper noun.

"What cowboy?"

"Not '*what*' cowboy, my dear. Cowboy, the man. He was Ora's second husband, and he's the key to the mystery of that poem. See what you can find out about him. And, Kay?" Viva narrowed her eyes.

"Yes?"

"Don't share any of this with anyone. If you do, doors will shut. I know that only too well."

Viva warned me twice. Concern teased my subconscious, but my excitement blocked its path. *The mystery keeps getting deeper. Where will it lead me?* I wondered.

"You have to give me something more to go on," I said. "I need to know his real name if you want me to research him."

I could see a hint of a smile playing on Viva's lips. "Cowboy's real name was Jesse Cole James, son of Jesse Woodson James and Emma Anders."

When I left, I sensed the beginning of one of the most interesting journeys of my life. My mother-in-law, I reflected, reminded me of a squirrel — one that gathered nuts for the last seventy years about Ora's life. Now, she wanted them cracked all at once and designated me to be the nutcracker.

I relished working on a mystery with Viva, an intriguing co-conspirator in the quest to solve the poem's riddle. Age might have robbed her of the physical ability to pursue the puzzle, but her mind remained lucid. If she believed this Cowboy would lead to the answer, then I believed it, too. The excitement of solving a puzzle stirred deep within me. Two years in Barber had not destroyed my love of a challenge. I secretly missed the intrigue of lab research and the mind-bending exercises required to produce results. However, the human element concerned me. I had never dissected the interactions of people. I preferred working with things that could not hurt you, like science and math. *Could I learn?*

# Chapter III

Early the next morning, I headed to Little Rock to dig up any information I could find on Cowboy, alias Jesse Cole James. I looked for the usual, birth and death certificates and any record of relatives I might talk to. I secured copies of both, as well as his World War II draft registration and the birth certificates of two of his children. I returned home and spread the documents out on the kitchen table.

The original handwritten documents had faded, making the copies hard to read. With a magnifying glass in hand, I set about gleaning facts on Jesse Cole James.

First, I looked at the death certificate. Ora Louvinna Price Townsend Hacker James reported that Jesse Cole James was born in Texas, had ten siblings, and stated his parents as Jesse W. James and Emma Andrews. I compared that information with his birth certificate. Very few things matched up. The issue date on the birth certificate read 1956, but they listed his birth date as February 12, 1882. He would have been seventy-four years old when it was issued. *Clearly, I must take everything I read with a grain of salt.*

The death certificate listed Miller County, Arkansas, as Cowboy's birthplace. The draft registration listed his birthplace as Houston, Texas, and the place of birth listed on his children's certificates was Plainview, Texas. What a mess. Errors on the old records abounded, and none of these connected in the least. I did not have the faintest clue how to move forward. Hopefully, Viva could steer me once again.

I waited until midmorning before approaching Viva. To my surprise, she anticipated my arrival. She brewed a fresh pot of coffee and placed two cups on the table.

*Did she look forward to seeing me?* I filled the cups, handed her one, and sat down next to her so we could view the papers together. Feeling like a schoolgirl who couldn't wait to share a secret, I began with a multitude of reported birthplaces ranging from Arkansas to Texas. I could not imagine how anyone could make sense of the conglomerate, but I knew she would try.

"Cowboy knew how to keep a secret," Viva said, nodding. The discrepancies hadn't surprised her in the least.

"He never shared more than he wanted you to know. He told no one — except maybe Ora — where he came from." Her eyes danced with amusement as she looked at me. "People would ask him where he was going, and he'd say, 'that way.' When they asked him where he came from, he'd say, 'back that way.' Sometimes, he'd just tell them it was none of their concern."

"Sounds cagey," I commented, sipping my coffee.

"As far as I can tell, he never lied." A half-smile curved her lips. "He talked in riddles, though, and you had to figure it out."

"Thanks a lot," I said, my tone sarcastic. "It's harder to solve riddles once all the people involved are dead." But, even as I said it, I knew I wanted to give it my best shot. I would do it because of Viva, but, more importantly, I would do it for me. I felt like a boxer who just re-entered the ring after a long absence, energized by the adrenaline of a mystery.

Would this poem pierce the invisible wall between us? I yearned to connect with her.

I put down my cup. "Viva, can you think of anything … any tidbit about Cowboy that might lead me in the right direction?"

"Well, here's what I believe," she said. "In some fashion, Cowboy was responsible for Ezra Hacker's hanging. I never thought for a moment that a young man with a son less than a few months old would abandon his wife and child. They might have had a spat, but abandonment? Jail? Suicide? My goodness, if you were serious, you would just lie and then leave in the middle of the night.

"And, look at Ora. She was fifteen years old when Ezra supposedly hanged himself. What could she possibly have done to make a young man prefer to die rather than return home?"

I had no answer. I could not imagine choosing suicide in any situation, much less the one she described.

Viva took a long swig of coffee and then set the cup carefully back down. "Kay, remember, the poem says Ora Price was the cause of it all. But, think about that! When Ezra died, her name was *Hacker*, not Price, and no one knew that better than her husband. I can't think of any law — old or new — that would put a man in jail for wife abandonment. Yes, they found Ezra Hacker hanging in that jail, but he did not hang himself, and he did *not* write that poem."

There you go. My mysterious suicide just took on the nuances of a murder. Viva made perfect sense.

"Do you remember when I told you about Ben Townsend's objections to a Christian burial for Ezra and how cold he was to Ora's mother, Ellie?" she asked. "Something was never right with that family."

She sounded emotional about it, so I asked the obvious question. "How did you get so entangled with these people?"

"Well, Ora was my closest friend, and I was her *only* friend. The first time I ever laid eyes on Ora, except through a keyhole, was the day of Ezra's funeral. He died on the nineteenth of December, don't you know, and they put him in the ground two days later. I sat quietly in the back, trying my best to be invisible. That's when I saw her come in the church with Ellie, holding a small baby in her arms. They walked real quick-like to the front of the church and sat in the first pew. Then they just sat and sat, waiting."

I got up and poured more coffee. "Thank you," said Viva, nodding. "Oh, Kay, I remember it so well. Ellie sitting there as stiff and still as stone. Ora looking like she was crying, but she never made a sound. The baby cried up a storm. So, I nipped up there and took him outside. They called him Little Joseph." After a short silence, she leaned forward and began to talk in a low, confidential tone. "You know what everybody was waiting for, don't you?"

"What?" I hadn't noticed until now that I was holding my breath. The story of the ill-fated teenage couple mesmerized me, and Viva sure made the most of every word. "They were waiting for the other mourners. But, only a few came. Not even Ben showed up ... just a few Hackers. Other than that, no one." She took a deep breath and exhaled slowly. "Papa preached the service, and Momma played 'Amazing Grace' on the organ. Short and sweet. When Ora came out, I could see she was in no condition to take care of the baby. I told her to go on, and she could pick him up later. That's how we became friends. She came for her baby and, after that, she came over a lot. Maybe she needed someone normal in her life."

"Why did they shun Ezra after he died?" I asked.

"Well, some people believed that suicide was a sin, so Ezra doomed himself to hell. Other people said they were afraid to show their faces at the church. After all, if Ezra didn't kill himself, then someone else did."

"What did Ora think?"

"I'm not sure she knew *what* to think. She believed she caused it — but she knew better than anyone that he abandoned *her*. She claimed she told him something she shouldn't have. Ol' Ben broke the news to her that they tossed Ezra in jail. The next day he was dead."

A smile crossed Viva's lips. "Ora tickled me," she continued. "She told me she prayed daily to the Lord for a man. Any man would do. Between you and me, Ora wasn't pretty. Plump as a brooding quail, she always twisted her hair into a knot at the nape of her neck. Even at sixteen, she looked matronly. Lordy, it had to be divine intervention for Ora to get a man. But, less than a year after Ezra died, she got her man … even if he arrived shot up and almost dead."

My coffee cup slipped through my fingers, landing with a clatter on the table. "What are you talking about? Who got shot?"

The smile never left Viva's lips. "It happened like this," she said. "Cornelia's husband Ben and her brother Bud Hooper were neighbors. They always seemed to be up to something. It wasn't friendship, 'cause Ben was *not* the kind of man to have friends. But, they were always up to something, like I said, and one night they pulled this man out of a boxcar and took him to the Hooper house. He was all shot up and bleeding. So, Ben sent Ora over there to take care of him."

"Who was it?"

Her eyes locked with mine.

"Cowboy," she said. "Ora spent every waking hour with him … her and Little Joseph, nursing him back to health. She tried to talk to him, but he made it clear he didn't want any conversation, and he never even seemed to notice the baby."

"Doesn't sound very romantic," I commented.

"Not very," Viva agreed. "And, as you can imagine, no one seemed more surprised than Ora when Ben informed her she had to marry this stranger when he was up and about. All she could say to me was that she had prayed for a man, and now she had one."

"For better or worse," I muttered.

Viva grinned in affirmation. "And, what a man! Over six feet tall with dark hair and blue eyes. I remember he always wore a starched blue shirt tucked in his jeans and polished boots. Quite striking in appearance. You know how some people have a way of dominating a room just by being there?" The question required no answer, but she waited for my nod before continuing. "That was Cowboy. He scared me a little, don't you know. He seemed cold and quiet like a copperhead. Pretty, but lethal. I would have preferred him to be more like a rattlesnake. At least they warn before they strike. Ha!" She laughed at her twisted humor.

"You mean Ora married a man she hardly knew?" I

thought arranged marriages stopped in the middle ages or happened only in foreign countries.

"Well, she didn't know much about him, but Cowboy told her one thing before the marriage. He looked her straight in the eye and told her that his father was Jesse *Woodson* James, and there would always be grave danger if she married him. He emphasized the middle name as if trying to ensure he would not be confused with any other man.

I gasped. "Did he mean Jesse James, as in the famous outlaw?" I had heard the name Jesse James all my life.

"I believe so. Ora was convinced Cowboy had the past of an outlaw. I'm sure coming into Booneville shot up and half dead helped."

This story became better and better. "What do *you* believe?" I asked her.

Viva took her time before answering, as though she chose her words with care. "I never questioned Ora. In her heart, she accepted what he told her."

Her answer did not satisfy me. I felt Cowboy carried more weight than just being the husband of Viva's best friend. But, she looked too tired for me to ask about it, and I wanted to go home to make notes and think a little more about Ora Price Townsend Hacker James.

The story fascinated me. *Had Ezra committed suicide, or did he die to conceal a secret? Who was Cowboy? How did he fit into Ezra's demise? Had Ora really caused her husband to hang himself?*

I decided to focus, first, on Cowboy and his parentage. Could he be the son of Jesse Woodson James? I kept that question with me the rest of the day, determined there would be answers in the morning.

# Chapter IV

I appreciate the value of a Big Chief tablet. Before laptops crunched and saved information with mindless keystrokes, I spent many hours in research labs arduously recording the data of each chemical trial by hand in a journal. Technology became a great boon to the research field, but something got lost in the shuffle as well. The tangible touch of a pencil connecting my fingers directly to my brain immersed me in a project in a way that escaped the scope of a keyboard. So, with studied deliberation, I listed what I knew in columns on a simple paper tablet.

| Name | Mother | Father | Birth Place | Birth Date |
|------|--------|--------|-------------|------------|
| Jesse Cole James | Emma Andrews | Jesse Woodson James | Houston, TX | Feb 13, 1882 |
| JC James | Emma Anders | | Plainview, TX | 1882 |

The real conflict seemed to be the place of birth and the mother's name. However, Viva told me repeatedly that Cowboy called his mother Anders, not Andrews, so

I wasted little time on that one.

The place of birth became a real mystery. I turned on my computer to learn more about how these locations stood in relationship to each other.

My interest focused on the distance between Houston, Texas, on the Gulf of Mexico, and Plainview, in the west part of the state. When I typed in Plainview, Texas, the screen stated there were six towns in Texas with the name of Plainview, and asked me to pick a county. That thought never crossed my mind. I should have known better than to make assumptions. I kept scrolling through the list of counties to choose from when Houston County leaped off the screen. Plainview, Houston County, Texas. Two anomalies melded into one plausible location. My excitement exploded. The first step in unraveling Cowboy's story revealed itself. If I truly found his birthplace, Emma could not be far away.

I turned once again to the internet. This time I looked for a person, not a place. This task proved a little more difficult. With many websites for genealogy, I narrowed my selection down to Ancestory.com and Genealogy.com. Each contained a wealth of information.

I poured over the census data, day after day, looking for the elusive Emma Anders. I felt myself reverting to old habits — drowning in my obsession to complete a task — to solve the puzzle. I sat before the computer in the morning and refused to leave my post except for food and bathroom breaks, partly to please Viva and partly to feed my deep-seated drive to conquer a challenge.

Darrell's job as a geologist for a local mining company often called him away for several days at a time. He loved roaming the Arkansas hills and getting paid for it. I used to dread these trips that would take him away, but now I relished the time I had to do my research. What a story I would have for him when he got home this evening.

I met Darrell at the door, brimming with more enthusiasm than I had felt in a long time. My words spilled out like rapid-fire, starting with the jail, then the poem, and finally, my visit with his mother. Life in Barber had been a little boring, at best, and I could hardly contain my excitement about the mystery of Cowboy and Ezra.

The joy I experienced with my tale faded swiftly as I watched his expression. Darrell lacked enthusiasm for my newfound pursuit. I could sense his displeasure each time I mentioned Cowboy's name. He ducked his head and looked away, obviously irritated with my every word. His lack of interest troubled me, but the siren call of the mystery overshadowed everything, including his feelings. I did not understand his reaction, but my frame of mind surprised me more. My willingness to ignore his obvious disapproval seemed foreign but real. I told myself I would soon find the answer and our lives would return to normal. I just needed a little time.

Darrell stood in the doorway with one arm clasped to the frame. When he finally spoke, his tone conflicted with the demeanor of the man I knew.

"What's for supper? Or are you too busy to cook?" he asked. No comment on my story. Instead, he changed the conversation completely and refused to look me in the eye.

Before I could answer, he stormed out the front door. I never saw this coming. My sweet, mild-mannered husband morphed into a sarcastic and, yes, mean-spirited person.

"Wait, a minute!" I ran after him. "What's the matter?"

"My problem is that I come home expecting a wife who is

happy to see me. Instead, you are consumed with Cowboy. You are wasting your time running after silly poems and dead men."

"That's unfair. I only work on it when you are away," I snapped.

"Leave it alone, Kay. I don't want Cowboy in my house!" His gaze dropped again.

I could not tell if he was pleading or commanding me to quit. My mind raced to Viva's warning, "Don't tell anyone. If you do, doors will shut." *Is this the first door, or is her rebuke playing with my mind?* I couldn't quit, but I didn't want to cause a rift between us either.

"I promise not to let Cowboy interfere with our lives, but please don't take this away from me."

I could see Darrell wavering.

"You don't know what you are getting into. I wish you would let the past stay in the past. I've told Mom the same thing. She listened until you came along. I love you both and don't want to see you hurt."

"I'll be careful. I won't talk to anyone except you and Viva."

"Suit yourself, but I don't want any part of it."

His decision didn't give me the permission I wanted, but we had a truce. I put the story away until the next time he left town.

A week later, I found another clue on the Ancestry website: Emma A. Anders, born 1867 in Marlin, Falls County, Texas. The details all matched my Emma.

I concluded Viva and I would have to go to Texas. I hoped she could make the long trip. My intrigue would not allow me to back up now, and only she knew what I needed to find.

Even with Viva's excitement about going, I admit her ability to make the trip concerned me. This elderly woman, who once stood a proud five-foot, three, had now shrunk to a mere five feet. Her skin hung loosely about her delicate frame. Her steps had an uneven, halted gait as she struggled to ignore arthritis that attacked her joints and bones. But, I could see the fire of determination in those watery blue eyes. Against Darrell's better judgment, we left early the next morning in my Jeep. Viva talked non-stop for the first hundred miles. Strangely enough, she seemed to strengthen as we progressed. I felt as if I was watching a butterfly emerge from a cocoon.

"I didn't remember how beautiful the countryside is," Viva said, as she looked out the window. "When my husband and I took trips, I took it all for granted. I traveled by myself after he passed, but I haven't seen this country in over ten years."

I never thought about her wanting to journey outside of Barber. I guess when people get older, we assume they just want to sit in their homes and wait to die. I felt awful that I had not taken Viva on a trip before.

"Where did you go?" I asked. I wanted to keep her talking. I wanted her to enjoy our time together.

"We went all over … that is until Darrell came along," she added.

"I guess you had to quit traveling when you got pregnant."

"Pregnant? Oh, Lordy, honey. I was never pregnant. I couldn't have kids."

My mind raced with the implications of her words. If she could not have children, then who were Darrell's parents? How did Viva fit in the picture? He called her "Mom." I had no reason to question it.

"Darrell's adopted. Didn't you know?" She said it as if we

were discussing the weather.

*NO! I didn't know. Why wouldn't he tell me something as important as that?*

"Oh, yeah," I said weakly. "I guess I don't remember all the details." I choked down the bile of resentment churning in the pit of my stomach.

"Let's stop for a minute to let me stretch my legs and go to the restroom. And, I sure could use something to drink."

I reluctantly stopped. My desire to pursue Darrell's saga waged a battle with my patience.

While Viva went into the convenience store, I filled the Jeep with gas. Soon she emerged with a bagful of candy bars and cans of soda. I glanced at the small brown bag of saltine crackers and cheese she packed to "tide us over." It remained untouched as we indulged in chocolaty Milky Way bars washed down with sweet strawberry soda. For just a moment, I felt like a child sharing a treat with her mother. I smiled despite my sour mood. Viva gave me my first gift.

The feeling passed quickly. Consumed by this new revelation, the minute we hit the highway, I needed to know more about Darrell.

"Tell me how you came to adopt him." I hoped I sounded nonchalant, but I struggled to contain myself.

"Why, he was Joseph's boy. You know, Ora's son. Ora was Darrell's grandma."

"Ora's *grandson*?" The words and soda spewed from my mouth.

"He hasn't told you anything, has he? Well, we've got lots of time so I will. You *need* to know." Her words seemed a little smug. *Does it amuse her that my husband kept secrets from me?*

Viva finished her chocolate and took one more swig of soda before she began.

"Remember when I told you about Cowboy? How he ignored Little Joseph from the beginning?" I nodded. "Well, it got nothin' but worse. He would cuff the boy for no good reason. Once, Joseph came to the house, a big welt across his back. When I asked what happened … he couldn't have been more than five at the time … he said he had touched Cowboy's prize fiddle." Viva shook her head. "When Cowboy got drunk, he could be very mean. I suspect he was drunk and playing his fiddle when Little Joseph got in his way."

My eyes teared. How could grownups be so cruel to children?

"What did Ora do about it?" Surely, a mother instinctively protects.

"Nothing! Absolutely nothing," replied Viva. "I think she feared Cowboy, so she just let it be."

I began to think about how Ora had chosen to anchor her life to the soul of another and hang on for the ride. First, her step-dad Ben, and then her husband Ezra. Finally, Cowboy. I asked myself if I were any different. Could I be guilty of doing the same thing with Viva and Darrell? Had I given up myself to please others? I suspected Ora and I to be much alike.

"Joseph left home at thirteen and went to live with his grandpa Hacker over in Magazine. I don't know if his life got any better, but he was with his own people. I think they treated him more kindly."

"So, was Joseph living in Magazine when Darrell was born?" I asked.

"No. Back in the twenties, times were really hard in Arkansas. No rain. No crops. A lot of folks just picked up and left. Off to pick crops in the 'Promised Land.' Joseph went with them."

"Then Darrell was born in California?"

"Yes. I really don't know much about what happened out there, but I do know Joseph married a lady, and they had two little ones. When Darrell was three, his mother and baby sister died in a house fire. Joseph worked the graveyard shift for some shipping company, so he wasn't home when the fire broke out. A neighbor saved Darrell, but everything else in the world burned to the ground." Viva fell silent.

Why had Darrell never shared this with me? I felt betrayed beyond words, but my curiosity demanded satisfaction.

"What caused the fire?"

"Joseph said the 'Hacker Curse' caused it, and that his papa's doings would haunt him until the day he died. I knew then that Joseph had just plain lost his mind. He handed me his baby boy and asked me to raise him. I thought he would want Ora to have him … but he said no."

"Then Darrell never really knew his father," I said.

"No, and we never heard from him again, either. A few years later, I got a letter from an asylum in Illinois saying Joseph had died."

So, Darrell's dad died in an asylum. His grandpa Ezra had hanged in jail, and his grandma Ora didn't want him. Darrell never mentioned these crushing events in his life. It seemed I did not know my husband at all.

The long trip and the hot afternoon sun tired Viva. She gave in to her drowsiness and slipped into a nap, giving me a chance to absorb the bombshells she lobbed at me today. My emotions danced dangerously close to the surface, threatening to derail my mission to unravel the mystery of Cowboy. I had much to think about and needed to get a grip.

The mysterious poem on the wall now entwined with my personal life. Darrell's entire existence was submerged in this saga of Jesse Cole James, and my quest hit a nerve that shot pain throughout his entire being. My commitment to the story surrounding Cowboy grew stronger than ever, but I would tread more carefully.

We arrived in Marlin, a tiny Texas town about seven miles east of the Brazos River. The large falls that disrupted the gentle flow of the river on its way to the marshy bayous on the Gulf of Mexico had served as the inspiration for the name Falls County. I thought we might make out better if we continued on to Waco for accommodations, but with both of us tired, we settled for the first motel we found and crashed for the night.

I thought Viva would sleep late the next morning, but the spirited old soul arose early. I heard her turn off the shower and, a few moments later, she emerged from the bathroom.

"Could you fix my hair in the back, dear? It gets so flat when I sleep on it, and I forgot to bring my silk pillow, don't you know? So, I am sure it's a mess."

The back of her hair pressed in and made the hair on the sides billow out like two ear muffs. I used my pick and fluffed and flattened until I had restored the perfect globe that framed her head. Then I walked to the motel lobby to pick up coffee and two blueberry muffins to tide us over, smiling all the way. I had successfully stowed my feelings of betrayal from yesterday. Besides, seeing her fuss about her appearance endeared her to me. Age had nothing on vanity. I hurried back with the makeshift breakfast, ready to continue our journey.

We made our first stop at the Falls County courthouse. The large Greek revival structure, embellished with concrete columns flanking the entrances, looked formidable. Steep stairs ramped up to the stately portals, creating a grand statement.

How would Viva ever make that climb? She must have shared my concerns because she quickly suggested that she wait on a shaded bench in the courtyard. I agreed and hurried to the clerk's office to do a record search for anything pertaining to the Anders family. It didn't take long to exhaust any clues the court records could supply. I made copies of old land records and hastily retreated to check on Viva. There she sat, just as I had left her. A woman of approximately the same age had joined her. They seemed to be engaged in a lively conversation.

As I approached, Viva introduced the woman. "Kay, I want you to meet Elizabeth Allen. Her parents were good friends of the Anders family."

*Good going, Viva!* I had been methodically searching for bones while she went straight for the flesh.

"It's so nice to meet you, Elizabeth." I gently touched the bird-like hand she extended in welcome.

"It's nice to meet you as well, my dear. I've heard so …" She stopped mid-sentence as Viva shot her a sideways glance.

"Elizabeth wants us to join her for lunch and visit for a while," Viva said, her voice matter-of-fact. She beamed at the prospect. "She lives at 1303 Anders Street, just up the hill. I told her we would pick her up there at one o'clock."

So, they had already struck a deal. I looked back and forth at the ladies, uncomfortable with the liaison. An elusive bond existed between these two women. Again, I peered through a windowpane of a world that did not belong to me. I resolved to find my way in.

# Chapter V

We had no problem finding Elizabeth's home in the small Texas town. A grand portico sagged with the weight of time, but the bones of the stately mansion clung to the charm of an old southern plantation.

Elizabeth met us at the door with the graciousness of a southern belle. Tightly curled gray hair framed her face like a soft bonnet. Two distinct, yet subtle, circles of rouge and pale pink lipstick complemented her fair complexion. She had prepared for company.

"I hope you don't mind, but I made some sandwiches for lunch. It's much easier than going out, and that way we can visit more," she said as she stepped into her house.

I felt a little uneasy. The house had a melancholy aura of a long-gone era. I could feel a sense of traveling back in time to the turn of the century. Not the most recent one at that. Viva appeared not to notice.

The time warp did not end at the front door. Tall windows,

sheathed in heavy damask drapes, threw deep shadows across the dimly-lit parlor. A slightly worn Victorian settee and two velvet wingback chairs anchored the hand-loomed carpet centered on the oak floor. An elegant roll top desk occupied the far corner of the room. The furnishings had been well cared for, but a mustiness lingered in the air.

Elizabeth and Viva moved to the dining room adjacent to the front parlor. I hastened to join them. I did not want to appear rude.

Three prim and proper place settings surrounded a platter of crust-less, triangular sandwiches at the far end of the enormous table. Crystal goblets filled with iced tea completed our noon fare. I slipped into the nearest chair and waited restlessly for the conversation to begin.

Viva sipped her iced tea before speaking. "It all looks wonderful, Bessie. I can't thank you enough for inviting us into your — "

She stopped mid-sentence, inhaling sharply as if to suck the words back into her mouth.

"I am so sorry. I shouldn't have called you Bessie. I'm not sure what I was thinking."

"Please," Elizabeth interrupted. "No apology necessary. Everyone calls me Bessie." She flapped her hands dismissively. "And, before you say another word, I want you to know, I love to reminisce about the past. Folks around here are bored with my stories. You just tell me where to begin, and I will see what I can do to help."

Viva pressed her hand to her heart, rolling her eyes heavenward. Her obvious relief seemed excessive for such a minor sin.

"We're here to find out about Emma Anders. Do you

know anything about her or her family?" I interjected. I needed to get the ball rolling, but I couched the reaction in the back of my brain.

Bessie nodded. "Yes, I do. That's one of my favorite stories. James Hammett Anders, Emma's daddy, is where *my* story begins. It's a long story, so bear with me. It can get confusing," she added. Her cheeks dimpled with delight at the thought of a new audience for her beloved tale.

I nibbled at a sandwich absentmindedly, my focus on Bessie. Her soft, honey-coated words, riddled with southern slang, required an attentive ear. I didn't want to miss a dang thing.

"James Hammett Anders worked for a man named Willis Lang in Mississippi. I think Papa told me he was the overseer of the Lang's property. Things weren't good for Willis in Mississippi, on account of no proper rainfall, so he sold his land and bought hundreds of acres on the Brazos Bottoms. That's what folks around here call the land along the Brazos River," she added, making sure we followed the story. "I expect it's the best acreage in the county. It was about 1854 when James brought seventy-five Lang slaves from Mississippi to Falls County by ox wagon. Falls County was only four years old, and Marlin just a village at the time. Willis bought a complete outfit for opening up a plantation: mechanics, farm implements, mule teams …" Bessie's words trailed off as she reached for her glass of tea.

I enjoyed listening to her soft, whispery voice with its slight southern accent.

Bessie took a dainty sip and then placed her goblet on a coaster. "It was a very exciting time. Papa said it was as if the deep roots of our southern plantations had been plucked up and replanted in the rich soil of Texas. Folks came by the wagonloads to Falls County. Marlin was booming. No one was more successful at running a plantation than Willis and James. But …" She paused, drawing out the last word as if to create drama.

It worked.

"What?" Viva and I exclaimed in unison.

Bessie smirked, obviously pleased with our reaction. "The more the plantation prospered, the less interested Willis seemed in running it. He left running the plantation to James while he went on scouting trips with a company of rangers out of Waco."

I struggled to show the appropriate amount of dismay at Willis Lang's obvious neglect of duty, but it must have satisfied Bessie's need for validation. She sipped again and continued. "When Governor Houston put out a call to all Texans to '*pursue, repel and punish marauding Indians that were plaguing our settlements*'," she said, curling her fingers where there were quotation marks in her narrative, "Willis was among the first to volunteer. I don't believe he ever saw any Indians, but I'm told he didn't seem to mind. He probably thought it was a great buffalo hunt." She placed a hand over her mouth to stifle a girlish giggle.

"It sounds like the sort of thing men do to amuse themselves," Viva said drily.

Bessie shrugged. "Be that as it may, Willis never married."

A silence hung over the room, as though we all contemplated the man who seemed to take life a little less seriously than womenfolk would have wanted.

"James had better fortune," Bessie said. "He married Miss Pauline Yarbrough from over in Smith County. Their families had known each other in Mississippi, and he had been taken with her for quite some time. Mama said she was small-boned and petite, almost like a china doll. With cornflower-blue eyes and silky blonde hair, every man in the county felt somewhat smitten with her."

I took another sandwich, imagining the porcelain beauty of Miss Pauline Yarbrough.

"Some say Willis never married because he, too, loved Pauline. I don't know that to be a fact. But, I do know that when little Ida was born, you would have thought it was Willis's child and not James's. He spoiled baby Ida to the point of shamefulness, and he lavished plenty of attention on Pauline, too. James never appeared jealous, but it sure makes one wonder."

The ticking of the mantel clock marked the passing of the afternoon like a metronome, keeping a slow and steady pace. The sound comforted me, like the rhythm of a heartbeat, a backdrop to Bessie's story. I wanted to get to the part about Emma, but I feared pushing her too hard.

"Does this mean you think Willis was Ida and Emma's father?" I realized how silly the words sounded as soon as I spoke them.

"Oh! Good heavens, no!" Bessie said. "Willis died before Emma was born. Now, Ida, that's a different story. Let me show you a letter Papa kept in his personal papers."

She went straight to the oversized roll-top desk in the far corner and, with little effort, produced a faded parchment letter written by hand and signed by none other than Willis himself.

"Read it aloud, dear," Bessie commanded.

Z. Bartlett
Cecera, New Mexico

Dear Sir:
Feb. 27, 1862

We met the enemy near Fort Craigg and gained a signal battle. Our victory was complete. The enemy was 3,000 strong with 7 pieces of artillery. The loss on their side was very great, full 300 killed and about 60 wounded. We took all their artillery. The charge upon the artillery was terrible, and what is astonishing, but few fell -- the greatest loss was on our little company, -- 9 were killed, to wit Isaac Marlin … 11 wounded …. None were severely wounded, but Mr. Bass, whose left arm is so completely fractured and shot to pieces that he was obliged to have it amputated this morning. He received 7 shots in all, and Jack Davis was also severely wounded. My own wound is dangerous. Those who are called to shed a tear over the fate of their relative or friend may have the consolation that it was not over a coward. The conduct of the company will elicit applause from friend and foe. Please send copies of this letter throughout the country that the friends may know who have fallen and who have been injured. Send one to James Anders, and tell him to kiss Ida a thousand times. I may not live to do so again.

Respectively yours,
Willis L. Lang

"You see, even in battle, Willis's thoughts were never far from little Ida," Bessie said.

I thought, but didn't say, his spelling could use a little work. "Did Willis live to kiss little Ida again?" I asked instead.

"No. Willis had terrible wounds, and they sent him to a hospital in Socorro, New Mexico. He is listed as a casualty of the battle of Val Verde … the truth is, he took his own life. He had his body servant bring him his revolver, and he shot himself. I guess the pain was awful, and he felt there was no hope of recovery," she said with a grim twist of her mouth.

"So, how does Emma come into this picture?" I asked. "The story appears to end with Willis's death." It was a lovely story, but the afternoon grew short, and there had been no mention of Emma.

"I told you Emma's story is long and complicated, dear. If I don't tell you the *whole* story, the pieces will make no sense. Now, as I was saying …" Bessie held out her goblet, and I poured more iced tea. "Thank you, dear. Now, where were we? Oh, yes. We were talking about Willis. He left little Ida a sum of $20,000 in his will, and he willed the plantation on the Brazos Bottoms to his cousin named Billingsley. James inherited nothing. I need not tell you how rich that made little Ida. At only three years old, she had more money than almost anyone in the county."

"What a ridiculous sum of money to bequeath to a child," I said. "I would have predicted that any inheritance from the Lang estate would have gone to James. Did he fight, too?"

"No, dear. James stayed home and managed the plantation for Willis. It seems as if every waking thought and action was solely for the benefit of his friend. When he died in March of 1862, a part of James died with him, I'm sure of that. James was independent and *not* much in favor of the war," she said, jutting her chin forward.

*Did Bessie disapprove of a man who refused to fight?* I wondered.

"But, no doubt, he felt a deep loyalty to his lifetime friend. Willis's death hit Pauline hard. As I said, that woman was too delicate. No stamina. Pregnant at the time, she insisted on naming her newborn son after Willis Lang. As much as James loved him, Pauline's determination to name their firstborn son after him stung."

"It seems a little inconsiderate of James's feelings, don't you know," said Viva.

Bessie didn't even give Viva a sideways glance. "Little Willis was the spittin' image of Pauline, and as frail as his mother, too. As a matter of fact, Pauline never recovered after his birth. Some said the loss of Willis stole her health. Others thought she lacked the strength for childbirth."

"It was more difficult back then," I murmured, aware I voiced a platitude, but it played better than shaking her and crying, *Get on with the story!*

"Either way," said Bessie, "her health declined, so James sent for Pauline's sister, Martha, to help her and the children. She arrived a few months after Little Willis was born and cared for Pauline until her death. When she died, James lost his joy for living but needed a wife for the sake of his children. He married Martha the very next year."

*Marriage for convenience appeared to be a common occurrence*, I thought. I had married later in life and solely for love. These people acted like they applied for jobs.

I glanced at Viva. She had listened with few interjections throughout the afternoon. Occasionally, she would bob her head ever so slightly, encouraging Bessie to continue her tale of Mr. Anders. I wouldn't say I became bored, but … *Where was Emma?*

"That's where Emma comes in," Bessie added, as though reading my mind. "Martha was Emma's mother."

I straightened up, eager now.

"Martha and Pauline were as different as day is from the night," Bessie went on. "James had lost his precious wife and, to be honest, her sister brought him little comfort. Yet, she tried to be a good mother to his children."

Bessie fanned her flushed cheeks with a napkin. "Hot this afternoon," she said out of the blue, "and we're out of iced tea. I'll get some water." At this, she shuffled off to the kitchen.

Viva leaned over and whispered, "Listen closely to the next part, Kay. Emma is crucial to Cowboy's mystery."

Before I could respond, Bessie returned with a pitcher of ice water and three more glasses.

"Okay, ladies. I'm ready. I believe we left off with Martha. Well, Ida never warmed up to her. She always called her 'Aunt,' even at only six years old when Martha became her stepmother. She cared even less for Emma.

"Little Emma was born in August 1867. She was James and Martha's only child. Ida didn't feel jealous of the baby, per se, but she didn't dote on her either. James had built his life around Ida and Willis. Pauline's sister and Emma had no place in their world."

Bessie glanced at her hands, folded neatly in her lap. "When Little Willis died two years later, the problem worsened. It was like two separate families living under one roof — one rich and one poor. Ida belonged to all the Marlin social circles. Emma did not. James made excuses, saying Emma was too young, or Martha did not possess the social skills Pauline had. Whatever the reason, it created a great divide." Bessie redirected her gaze to me, gauging my reaction.

"I can imagine," I said, feeling true sympathy for these people whose stories I had just started to learn. I hoped my answer met her expectations.

"How ironic for Ida to look more like Martha, with her big-boned frame, while Emma wound up petite and blonde like Pauline. When Emma blossomed in her early teens, Ida felt terribly envious of her. Martha maintained an indifferent attitude, but Emma rebelled."

"How on earth could people endure under such circumstances?" I asked. Death, indifference, and jealousy seemed to torment this family.

Viva answered this time. "People endure far worse."

Bessie picked right back up without acknowledging Viva's statement. "Ida returned home from finishing school before completing her senior year to marry a man named Lysis Chilton," said Bessie. "She married a very socially acceptable man, but you couldn't contain the rebellious streak in Emma. She took up with a man by the name of Redmond. Nice looking man with an easy, joking manner she couldn't resist. He only stayed a few short weeks, and he left Emma with child. I guess some things never change."

Again, Bessie's disappointment in the male species shone through. I could not say I blamed her.

"Ladies, let's leave it there for the evening," Bessie said. The telling had clearly tired her, and glancing at Viva, I saw she had wilted, too.

We drove the short distance back to the motel in silence. When we got to our room, Viva pulled a small box of papers from her suitcase and placed it on the bed. She gently removed a document, brittle with age, from her stash and held it squarely in front of my face. "Here, read this."

The State of Texas {County of Houston}

Affidavit

BEFORE ME, the undersigned authority, a Notary Public in and for Houston County, Texas, personally appeared Mary M. James, of Houston County, Texas, known to me to be a reputable person over 21 years of age of sound mind and body who deposes and states that, My name is Mary M. James, widow of William Martin James, deceased. My husband passed away in August 1947. My father was Joe Christi, he married Mary Louise Pate (my mother), and I was born not far from where I live now on January 3, 1867. I married Wm. M. James.

When I was about 10 years old, a man calling himself Jesse Redmond came to our house and stayed. He was hunting a place to rest up and hide out for a while. While with us a few weeks, he helped us pick cotton and do other work about the place which was on the Neches River. I had many opportunities to get a good look at this man who wore long hair, which was more or less wavy, he had blue eyes, fair complexion. I recollected then that he had left us a steel bulletproof jacket on the cotton wagon when my brother carried him to Lufkin, Texas. We found an identification card in the jacket naming him as Jesse James. My brother carried him on to Lufkin, and he sent a gallon of whiskey back with my brother for my father. I do not recall seeing him any more until the week of April 8, 1948, at which time this same man came for a week's visit with my son and his wife. I would be willing to swear that this man, going by the name of J. Frank Dalton, is the same man we knew years ago as Jesse James alias Jesse Redmond.

Signed: _____
Mary M. James

I held the proof I needed in my hands. An affidavit proclaiming the legendary Jesse Woodson James had once assumed the name of Jesse Redmond.

My mind leaped back to the Redmond from Bessie's story, whose child Emma bore. This had to be the same man. Coincidence could not dovetail the affidavit from Houston County, Texas, and Cowboy's story from Barber, Arkansas to the exact same place and time in history. A small step forward, but a step indeed, in the journey to prove Jesse Cole James could be the illegitimate son of Jesse Woodson James.

The 'find' pleased me, but Viva's actions continued to perturb me. Why hadn't she shared this before?

"Viva, this is an important clue. What else do you have in your brain — or box — that I need to know?"

"I'm sorry, Kay. I should have shared it with you sooner, but …"

"But what?"

"But … well, I told you Cowboy talked in riddles. The clues are in riddles. Almost nonsense to some. Nobody wants to entertain a twist in history that upsets their applecart, and I am here to tell you this story will do just that." Her eyes locked with mine. "I wanted you to believe in the story enough to continue. Not toss it aside as a crazy woman's ranting. But, remember, Kay, truth is the truth, even if no one believes it. Are you there yet?"

I had my doubts. How could I be "there yet?" In any case, here I sat, hundreds of miles away from home, in the middle of the Texas prairie. "Yes," I said, not sure what that affirmation meant.

Her eyes brightened. "All right. I will tell you what Cowboy said about his life before he came to Barber. He told Ora he was born in Plainview, Texas, and that he grew up near west Texas. He always said he'd gone to the monkey rhyme school, played with Joe Robles, and he had a redheaded sister named Mary. He told the family he had ten siblings, but that he was the youngest and the only one to keep the James name."

*Okay*, I thought. Cowboy said he was born in Plainview, Texas. I found Plainview in Houston County. Mary M. James provided her affidavit in Houston County. The Neches River she refers to is the northeast border between Houston and Cherokee counties. This still fits.

"What do you think about the west Texas statement Cowboy made?" I asked. If Cowboy were referring to the Plainview in west Texas, my theory would unravel.

"It's not what I think, dear — it's what I *know*. Cowboy

wasn't referring to a region of Texas. West is a small town just north of Waco. We passed it coming in from Dallas to Marlin." She beamed like a million fireflies blinking in the night sky. "It's just a wide spot in the road."

Oh! West, Texas, was a town. I could accept that, but the monkey rhyme school would be tough. Too much information flooded my mind. My brain needed time to percolate all the details. I told Viva I felt tired, and we could discuss this in the morning. We made quick work of getting ready for bed, but once there, I could not sleep. I believed my research on Emma Anders had brought us to Marlin, but Viva had already known about West, Texas. I could not be sure if I led her here or if she had masterminded the trip to Marlin, the crucible of Cowboy's origin.

"Don't forget, we are going to the Brazos Bottoms in the morning." Viva's voice startled me out of my drowsiness.

"The Brazos Bottoms?" I asked. "I don't remember making plans to go there."

"I'm sure we talked about it. Maybe you were out of the room. Anyway, we are picking Bessie up early so we can get around before it gets too hot," she said nonchalantly.

I drifted back to sleep, convinced I had been jay hooked again.

# Chapter VI

"Rise and shine," Viva chirped. She snapped the room-darkening curtains to the side. Bright shafts of sunlight assaulted my eyes, jolting me from a deep sleep. I blinked several times to bring the room into focus.

"What time is it?" I croaked.

"It's almost six-thirty, girl. Time to get cracking."

She had donned her best brown cotton dress with nylon hose rolled up to the knees. Black Quaker style shoes anchored her ample feet solidly to the floor. *Today must be special to her*, I mused as I watched her fuss about, gathering her purse and a serviceable straw bonnet. Viva looked her Sunday best.

"Where are we going, and why so early?"

"The Brazos, Kay. Remember? I told you last night," she said, waving her hands so fast I thought she would take flight.

My brain kicked into gear. I remembered. She threw out a tidbit about a trip to the Brazos just as we turned in last night.

"And it gets hotter than a firecracker here in the afternoon.

Now, let's go."

Impatience boiled just below the surface of her skin, flushing her cheeks to a bright red.

Her tone irritated me. I yanked on a pair of jeans, a tee shirt, and tennis shoes and pulled my hair into a ponytail. My appearance for the trip to the Brazos Bottoms did not concern me one iota, and Viva's concerned me even less. Her hair, normally a perfect dome, listed to one side. *No time to poof and puff this morning*, I rationalized with a tiny pang of guilt.

"I'm ready. Let's get cracking," I said with a touch of sarcasm.

"Better grab a hat."

"I'm good," I answered. Besides, I did not own a hat.

Bessie must have shared Viva's sense of the occasion. She emerged from her portico decked out in the attire of a socialite; white Capri pants, paired with a shiny turquoise blouse and white sandals, that would dazzle the most discerning eye. A large-brimmed hat with a scarf tied around the chin and oversized sunglasses completed her ensemble. She glowed with the aura of a refined southern belle coupled with the Hollywood glamour of the forties. I watched as she descended the wobbly stairway with the grace of a ballerina, defying her advanced age. Stunning.

She planted herself in the seat behind me, and off we went. The Lang Plantation lay on the Marlin-Waco road, about seven or eight miles west and north of Marlin. Few used this old road after the state built Highway 7. Bessie insisted we take this route. Against my better judgment, we took off on the poorly maintained side road. The rough asphalt lane became more and more narrow the farther we drove. Deep potholes jostled the Jeep, and us, as we rattled down the road to our destination.

The asphalt turned to dust, and the dust turned to muck, as we got closer to the river. I shifted into four-wheel drive and kept going. Bessie had picked well. The flat prairie farmland slowly gave way to the thick timberland that formed a ribbon of green along the river. Tall trees spread overhead and created a shady canopy over the road, by now little more than a trail. The musty smell of damp soil mixed with the sweet piney scent of the forest in this fertile retreat. Finally, we reached the Brazos Bottoms.

The road ran parallel with the river, but the dense foliage masked the rolling waters. We must have traveled over five miles before I could see the sandy banks of the river peeking through the dark green canopy. Around the next corner, the road flattened into a broad clearing, surrounded by weathered and rotting shacks encircling a large plantation equally ravaged by time.

I turned off the ignition and helped Viva and Bessie out of the car. Now, I could understand Bessie's choice of attire as I watched her make her way to the front of this rambling structure. She paid homage to the grandeur of the way of life that had once existed in this Eden sequestered deep in the heart of the Brazos.

I remained quiet, as did Viva, waiting for Bessie. Finally, she turned to us.

"Come on," she said.

She led us to the front veranda, where she opened what remained of the two large double-hinged doors. As they swung open, we could see the skeletal frame of the beams and timber. Even though the house had been abandoned for years, I felt like an intruder.

Bessie, however, looked quite comfortable as she led us through the historic plantation. The stairway to the second story had missing planks, making it impassable, but I could see portions of the rooms through holes in the ceiling. Bessie's tour ended on the back porch where she sat down at the top of a large stone stairway, which led to a once-grand courtyard. Viva and I followed suit.

"It is just as you described it, Bessie."

Viva had now confirmed my suspicion that the two women already had conversations about this place.

"Okay," I said. "Just what is going on that I don't know about?"

"Kay, what I told you last night was the truth," Viva said. "I just didn't tell you everything. I felt it would be better if, together, Bessie and I shared the information we worked on over the last two decades."

I gawked at her. *So Bessie and Viva knew each other after all. I should have known when she called her Bessie during our first visit. But how? And, why did they hide this from me?*

"May I ask why you kept me in the dark?" I directed my question toward Viva.

Ignoring the question, this new Viva raised her chin and looked down her nose at me. "Kay, are you listening?"

I nodded.

"As I told you before, Ora and I were best friends. After Cowboy, alias Jesse Cole, died, I wanted to prove his story. Her life had always been hard. She lost her real father at a young age and suffered through those awful years with Ben Townsend. Her first husband hanged himself at nineteen, and her marriage to Cowboy was a trial. But, the hardest part of all was the burden her children inherited from Jesse Cole.

They grew up knowing their father as the son of a famous outlaw. They each suffered for it, but that's another story." She shifted her position. "Cowboy's death freed me to find the truth and share it with her boys in hopes it would help them understand why they grew up the way they did. I wanted them to realize all their father's legacy meant." She sighed and exchanged glances with Bessie. "Ora didn't live long enough to uncover the truth for her children. But, I promised myself I would do everything in my power to validate Cowboy's story. That's not an easy task for an old woman."

Her vibrant passion could not merely be an interest in Ora's boys. I suspected Darrell's and Joseph's past figured deeply in her need to unravel these secrets. Viva could not be judged by what met the eye.

"And that's why you need me?" I asked.

"When Ora died, she left me all of her documents and papers to help in my search. That's what I carry in the box. I began by writing to the courthouse in Falls County, asking for information about Emma Anders. Bessie's the one who wrote back. Over the years, we've both worked on this project, Bessie, from his birth forward and me from his death back." She smiled at her friend. "We had never met in person, but when you offered to go to Texas, I wrote Bessie a letter."

*So, it was no accident we ran into her in Marlin,* I thought. "Why didn't you tell me? You know you can trust me." I felt more than a little hurt.

"I told you last night, it was important you knew enough to believe before I dumped the entire story on you. It's easy for people to think a person my age has dementia." Her serious manner changed abruptly to one of amusement. "You must admit, this isn't a story you'd tell people to convince them of your sanity." She chuckled. "My own son thinks I'm crazy. He doesn't approve of my obsession with the story. When you came along all excited about the hanging of Ezra Hacker, I hoped I had an ally." She reached over and squeezed my hand. "I wouldn't be here in Texas if it weren't for you."

Viva's affectionate gesture seemed insincere. She used me from the start.

"Why didn't you tell me you knew Bessie?" I accused her. "You planned to meet her all along."

"Darrell doesn't approve of our friendship. If I told you earlier, you might have let it slip."

The explanation seemed flimsy at best. *Why would Darrell not approve?* It crossed my mind that Viva only shared enough to get her way. Everything else she knew, I had to find out on my own. But, given my current status with Darrell, I could not afford to add fuel to the fire. I let it go.

I agreed about the 'crazy' part. If she had told me all of this before I saw the poem and had a mission of my own, I would no doubt have sided with him. "Are you two finally ready to let me in on the whole thing?" I asked.

Bessie cleared her throat. "Dear, you need to trust us. We've researched this for decades. There's still too much to tell in one sitting."

The temptation to take Viva's box and rummage through it tugged at me, but I had relationships to consider: hers and mine and mine with her son. I took a deep breath. "Okay, tell me about the Brazos."

Now, I knew the second reason Bessie's attire included a broad-brimmed white hat and sunglasses. She looked as cool as a cucumber. I, on the other hand, melted in the heat. I made a mental note to buy a hat.

"Well … where to begin?" Bessie mused.

Once again, I could see her slipping into the bygone world on the Brazos, one riddled with decay but still resplendent in all its glory. Her accent assumed a southern drawl, and her voice became whispery again as she began anew.

"You can't understand Jesse Cole unless you understand the Brazos. I brought you here for a reason. I wanted you to see how grand life on the Brazos Bottoms was until the Great War, which my papa used to call the War of the Lost Cause. This plantation, known as Rosebud Falls, sat at the base of the Brazos Bottoms and was owned by the Isaac Martin family. We're just below the falls and next to the Lang plantation I told you about yesterday. The Martins were strong southern sympathizers, and Isaac wintered Quantrill's troops here during the Civil War."

My mouth dropped open. "You mean Quantrill, as in Quantrill's Raiders?"

"None other," she replied. "He came during the winters to rest his men. They'd camp right here on the banks. Do you see those slave shanties?" She pointed to a dilapidated row of small, rectangular shacks that bordered the ribbon of water. "They would build their fires and pitch their tents between those shanties and the main house."

"Looks desolate," I said.

"At least there was no shortage of food." Bessie laughed. "These woods were full of deer and turkey. All kinds of wild game made its way to their tables as they awaited their return to the war."

"So, Falls County served as a haven for Confederate soldiers?" I asked.

"More than that, dear. Our people welcomed them as if they were their own sons or brothers or husbands seeking refuge from the rages of battle. Papa would often tell of the carpet dances they held in this very house in honor of Quantrill's men."

"Carpet dances?" I'd never heard the term.

"Oh, yes. They rolled up the carpets in the house to make room for a dance. The musicians, mostly slaves, played until the wee hours of the morning. They built their instruments … often fiddles made from gourds. But, the music was delightful, and everyone danced until all hours of the night. Neighbors came from all around, bringing large baskets of food and drink …" Her voice trailed off as she tilted her head and arched her feathery brows.

"The drink would sometimes cause a problem," she stated sternly, but delight still twinkled in her eyes.

"Papa loved to tell about the time the men got liquored up and smashed the gourd fiddles. But, that didn't stop the dance. They just picked up tin pans and beat them with wooden spoons as the couples twirled around the floor."

It sounded lovely … for everyone but the slaves.

Bessie didn't seem to find anything wrong with the situation. "Many of these very same Confederates returned to our beloved Texas after the war. Their lives and homes destroyed, we offered them a new beginning. Several of Quantrill's guerillas made their homes in and around Marlin in the years that followed."

I looked out beyond the shanties. I could imagine it *all*.

"Back then, outlaws and riffraff filled these woods," Bessie said. "Isaac told Papa you could hear the bloodhounds yelping and barking at fugitives running from the law. Quantrill's men formed their own vigilante party and cleared these parts out. They were the only law in the Bottoms. They took care of those who took care of them, and they took care of their own. This included the illegitimate son of Jesse Woodson James. Jesse Cole was raised here."

*About time his name came up again,* I thought as these two old ladies skirted around the truth. Bessie, genteel in both dress and manner, spoke of carpet dances as if she had attended one last evening, yet her only knowledge came from the stories passed down by her papa, and even *he* would have been too young to know many of these stories first-hand. The family lore sure had a strong hold on her.

On the other hand, Viva was a no-nonsense Arkansawyer. She dressed plainly, and her tightly curled hair made her face look sharp and severe. Her husband had made his living on the river. After he died, she constantly struggled to feed her family.

Yet, these two women joined forces in a decades-old search to establish the identity of Cowboy. One offered the beginning of his life, the other the end. I guessed my job would be to tie these threads together to complete the life of Jesse Cole James.

The relentless sun reached the top of the sky and beat down on us. We had to return to Marlin. I encouraged the ladies to get back into the car before we all succumbed to heatstroke.

# Chapter VII

*Phew!* Packed with travel, people, and stories, the last three days left me no time to think. I needed a break. Bessie and Viva's endless chatter continued until I dropped them off at Bessie's home. I wanted some time to myself, and I could think of no better place to process the recent events of my life than Rosebud Bend; this beautiful, haunting oasis in the Texas prairie drew me back to its solitude.

As I drove along the winding dirt road, my mind floated back to my past. Independent by necessity and a loner by choice, I sought my own counsel and "flew under the radar" until I found the answers I looked for. I learned this as a child, and it served me well.

Mother had never been fond of children. The burden of pregnancy, coupled with two very young offspring, appeared more than she could handle. It fell to my father to raise my older brother and me. Dad worked as a chemical engineer. He spent long days grinding out a living for a wife and three kids. Little time remained for my brother and me, but he gave us all he had. I remember standing on the front porch with my brother, decked out in swimsuits, towels tied about our waists, fingers crossed that Dad would arrive home in time to take us swimming. More often than not, night came, and the expected trip to the pool postponed once again. But, he tried. He pulled out the erector set or the checkerboard in the evenings to make amends for our disappointment, hiding his weariness.

Mother, on the other hand, spent her time caring for the baby. Any request that interrupted her routine irritated her. Curt replies of "Not now" or "Wait until your father gets home" ended all conversation. My brother and I survived in our own private world. Dad stood at the center of this universe, while mother hovered in the background. Yes, men anchored my sense of wellbeing, but my mother left an emptiness still unfilled. Perhaps this made my relationship with Viva more important to me.

I turned to books or tasks to escape my lack of connection with people. This trait served me well as I sailed through high school and then college to get my degree in chemistry. When I taught at the University of Arkansas, I interacted well with the students, but never formed lasting personal bonds with anyone. Until Darrell.

An easy-going, fun-loving, educated man, Darrell refused to take himself too seriously. The total opposite of me. I guessed losing his wife made him appreciate living. Darrell topped the list as the best thing that ever happened to me. I did not want to lose him.

On the other hand, this challenge of Jesse Cole consumed me. My choice in puzzles lacked discrimination. Chemical research or a silly poem held equal allure; they hooked me either way. But, I had to balance my drive with my love of Darrell, or I might lose both. I could turn the Jeep around, pick up Viva and head home, or continue driving to Rosebud Bend.

I rounded the corner that opened into the plantation.

This time I toured the grounds at a snail's pace. I strolled under the giant magnolia tree full of white waxy blooms and smelled the tangy fragrance of the mimosas that permeated the air. I could easily imagine a carpet dance in the main hall and leisurely visits on the veranda that surrounded the house.

I proceeded down to the slave shacks lining the river. The small rectangular boxes that once housed black families were barely four hundred square feet. These shacks sat on foundations of sandstone meant to give some elevation if the Brazos spilled over its banks.

As I approached the entrance to the nearest shanty, I tripped on a flat sandstone boulder etched with unusual markings reminiscent of hieroglyphics. Carvings resembling turkey tracks encircled a crudely chiseled figure of a badger. I didn't know what any of it meant. *Darrell would love this rock*, I thought. The perfect peace offering. Although large and heavy, I knew the rock would go with me.

I backed up the Jeep as close to the stone as I could. With a large stick and a smaller stone, I created a fulcrum and lever. I pushed and worked at it until I freed the rock from the soil. Drenched in sweat and out of breath, I still had to get the stone into the Jeep. I made a ramp to the trunk of the car using a large wooden plank I found leaning against a nearby cabin. Little by little, I worked the stone up the ramp, finally making it to the top. I had my prize. Excitement bubbled up as I returned to Marlin to share my good fortune with Viva.

I found Bessie and Viva in the parlor, surrounded by small piles of paper. Suppressing my curiosity about their doings, I coaxed them out to the Jeep and opened the trunk in a real "ta-da" moment. Bessie's mouth dropped, and her eyes widened in horror. I turned to Viva who shared the same expression.

"Shut the trunk *now*," Bessie ordered.

*What? It's not like I presented them with a bag of copperheads.* Nevertheless, I did as they said.

"Take it back! Take it back this minute!" she ranted. This sweet southern lady turned into a shrieking shrew right before my eyes.

Viva acted calmer, but no less firm. "Load up," she said. "You are taking the rock back to Rosebud Bend."

Her words pushed my patience to the breaking point. My jaw locked as I clenched my teeth to keep from saying words I could not take back. I did as they commanded.

The trip seemed eternal. When I rounded the same corner for the third time in one day, I breathed a long sigh of resignation. I started to reverse the process I had completed earlier but stopped in my tracks. Instead, I opened the hatch of the Jeep and removed the spare tire from its well. The stone fit perfectly. I needed this stone to solve the mystery of Cowboy. My years of training in science overshadowed wanting to please Viva. I would not fall into this whirlpool of emotions. I would "fly under the radar" again.

At this point, I wanted nothing more than to go home to Darrell and forget this crazy chase to decipher the meaning of a poem written almost a century ago. Deceived for days, and now chastised by two elderly women I hardly knew, my afternoon for rest and relief exploded into a full-blown battle of wills I did not understand.

The ride back to town could not be over soon enough. No more brouhaha for me. My intrigue and determination to complete a task wrestled with the resentment of being denied full access to the information Bessie and Viva shared. I would head home tomorrow, Viva in tow or not.

When I arrived at Bessie's house, I spied Viva and her perched on the front porch swing. I expected them to scatter like hens when a fox enters the chicken coop. However, when I pulled into the drive, Bessie approached the Jeep.

She caressed my shoulder. "Come in for a while, dear."

Bessie seemed totally disinterested in my current disposition, but Viva sensed my frustration and laid low. She didn't move. I could tell she hesitated to influence my actions. I glared at Bessie with visible belligerence. She nudged me and repeated her request. Not raised to be rude to my elders, I also did not want to offend Viva, so I mustered all the composure I could and consented.

The parlor exhibited the same disarray. I scooted a small pile of papers to the side and sat down on the Victorian settee. Viva and Bessie drew the two wingback chairs and planted themselves side by side in front of me.

"I know my actions seemed a little harsh today," said Bessie. "But, Rosebud Bend is sacred to those of us whose families fought for the Confederacy. Yes, we lost the battle, but we didn't lose the war … until 1916," she explained.

Viva took over. "Our soldiers went underground to protect the treasures they stole from the Yankees during the war. They never missed a chance to steal, rob, or loot from the Union and her allies during and after the war. They hid gold and the jewels they took in caves and abandoned mine shafts.

Sentinels, as we called them, guarded our stashes, waiting for the day the South would rise again. They marked the locations with the secret codes of the Knights of the Golden Circle carved into stones. That's what you found today. The mark of a sentinel for the KGC."

My head spun with this new information that flew in the face of conventional history. Could I sort it all out? The answer echoed a definite *yes*. Truth is the truth, even if no one believes it. I knew I could not give Darrell the stone that carried the mark of sentinels. He would not approve.

Before I said anything, Bessie added, "Jesse James headed up the KGC, which held close ties with Quantrill's army. Jesse Cole was a sentinel."

I leaned back in the settee and crossed my arms over my chest. "All right," I said. "I've got some questions."

The ladies answered my questions as the muggy afternoon passed us by, but I doubted they were completely honest with me. I took notes, but I really wanted to run to the nearest library with a computer and research the validity of these stories. I needed to verify Quantrill's men came to Marlin, that Jesse Cole grew up in the Brazos, the real existence of the KGC … the list seemed endless. When we parted for the evening, I planned for Viva to spend the next day with Bessie while I went on the hunt.

Research topped my list of fortes. I could spend hours combing records and documents, looking for clues. My focus on any task requiring patience and perseverance proved nothing short of rabid. I waited for the Marlin library to open at 10:00 the next morning.

Placing Quantrill and his men in Marlin Falls County, Texas, ranked high in my order of business. Even with my practiced Googling skills, it took hours to garner any information worth keeping. Finally, I landed on the USGENWEB site and drilled down Texas and Falls County. The Falls County webpage listed "Stories of Pioneers" on the menu. I clicked on it. A list of personal stories from the Falls County area appeared.

When I searched deeper, I landed on a site called "American Life Histories: Manuscripts from the Federal Writer's Project, 1936-1940." During the Great Depression, writers collected pioneer stories as a part of the Works Progress Administration.

The Falls County page contained thirteen stories, so I started reading from the top. The stories entertained me, but offered little to my mission until I reached, "Interview with Mr. Leroy Deam." My eyes, tired from hours of reading on the internet, still riveted on Mr. Deam's story, beginning with page two.

Folklore – White Pioneers
File No. 2240
Miss Effie Cowan PW
Page No. 2


"In the days before there were two communities of Odds, Stranger, Eureka, or the other little settlements on Blue Ridge, or close by, the country was part prairie, part lowland, part timber, surrounding the ridge. I can recall as a boy, how we used to roam over the wooded part, up and down the creek, hunting for birds of all kinds and wild turkeys and hogs. We learned the lore of the birds and the woods; to understand the wildlife was part of our education. It was our delight to listen to the talk of older men as they discussed the latest politics of the day, or the latest hanging, or the newest committee of Vigilantes that was organized to help the officers see to it that the law was upheld. For, at that time, law enforcement was yet in its infancy in Texas.

This organization was known as "Quantrill's Men," who were bushwhackers during the Civil War, had some members that lived after the war in our little town Marlin, Texas. There were three or four whom my father knew well. These were Major Swann, a lawyer of Marlin, Stump Ashby, another lawyer, and Professor Lattimore, father of the late Professor John Lattimore, who was at one time the County School Superintendent of Falls County. After the Civil War ended and the days of Reconstruction required the best of men to help uphold the law, there was a committee of men formed called Vigilantes.

These men who had belonged to Quantrill's Organization were among the first to make Texas unsafe for criminals. The course of the law would be so often delayed and not enforced 'cause many a man had to be dealt with without recourse to a trial by jury. I remember that in our community, there was an example of this. It was the hanging of one of the neighborhood men, Milt Brothers, who was accused of cattle theft ...

The article continued, but I had what I wanted. The story mirrored what Bessie had shared.

The big question — where to go from here? I believed Quantrill's men had settled in Marlin, and Jesse James had been a member of Quantrill's band. But, just how did Jesse *Cole* fit in?

I had more work to do, but the hours had slipped away from me. It was time to retrieve Viva.

When I arrived at Bessie's, I found no trace of my ladies in the house. *Where on earth could two elderly women go?* I sat on the front porch stoop and waited for a time without end. Flies buzzed about my face and arms, biting my sweaty skin at any opportune moment. Great. I lost Darrell's mother, and these pesky flies were punishing me for it.

Finally, around dusk, a timeworn Chevy Impala marked Marlin Cab Service pulled into the driveway. Viva and Bessie emerged, laughing and talking together like two old friends on an outing.

"Where have you been?" I snapped. Exhaustion and hunger made my temper flare.

Both ladies halted. I could tell by their disheveled appearance that they felt tired, too, but a look of pure joy glowed on their faces.

"We've been to the Spunky Flat schoolhouse!" Viva replied, grinning from ear to ear.

I racked my brain to determine the significance of the Spunky Flat schoolhouse. What an absurd name for a school, anyway.

Viva laughed. "Spunky – Monkey. Don't you get it? Cowboy went to the monkey rhyme schoolhouse. We found it. Well, actually, Bessie found it. But, anyway, we found Cowboy's school."

"I feared that would be the hardest of Cowboy's riddles

to solve. But, Bessie did it," Viva said, patting her friend on the back.

"Papa had a neighbor who used to talk about Spunky Flat," Bessie explained. "He said he lived between Big Creek and Brushy, just east of Marlin, and that they had an old schoolhouse there. It's still standing. Viva and I saw it today. It's an old hay barn now, but it's still there." She sounded out of breath. "He said the kids called it the monkey rhyme school. I just know it is Cowboy's school!"

# Chapter VIII

I hated to leave this vast expanse of wild prairies and cowboy lore known as East Texas, but the time came to go home. My mind accepted the Brazos as the crucible of Cowboy's infancy. With Emma Anders as his mother and Jesse Redmond, aka Jesse James, as his father, Jesse Cole spent his childhood in Plainview, a tiny little town clinging to the edge of Houston County. West, Texas — a town, not a direction — and the monkey rhyme school existed. While Cowboy did not lie, he sure made the truth hard to find.

I lifted our luggage into the truck, covering the wheel well to hide the stolen rock. Viva dilly-dallied this morning. She finally emerged with her shoebox of clippings tucked under her right arm and a heavy black purse slung over her left shoulder. She ambled toward me. I feared arthritis slowed her down, but her somber expression let me know more than achy bones pained her.

"I don't think we're done here, Kay." She screwed up her

brow and pursed her thin lips. "I have called Bessie a friend for twenty years, but I've only seen her for two days. Only *two days*," she repeated.

Puddles of tears brimmed in Viva's eyes, fading the watery-blue pupils to steel grey. Viva never acted like this.

"We will stop by and visit Bessie for a few minutes before we leave town," I said.

That idea seemed to pacify her. A weak smile replaced the grimace.

As I pulled into the drive, I saw two pieces of luggage perched on the top step next to Bessie. Dressed to travel, she beamed in a mint-green, linen sundress and white sandals, along with her customary large sunglasses. Bessie, our faded but beautiful southern belle, planned to go with us. Inside I seethed. *They set me up.*

The return trip to Arkansas bore no resemblance to the one on our way to Texas. Viva insisted on sitting in the back seat with Bessie so as not to waste a moment of the trip. I frequently stopped, as asked, but mainly let my mind drift as I sifted through the revelations of the past few days. Thoughts swirled in my head like a carousel, round and round, never stopping: the Brazos, a crumbling antebellum mansion, Cowboy, Bessie and Viva huddled in the back casting furtive glances my way, and Darrell. *Why did he hide his adoption from me? Are there more secrets?* The incessant spinning in my head harmonized perfectly with the hum of the road as the miles passed.

We arrived at Viva's farm at dusk. The rambling two-story frame house lacked the grandeur of Bessie's home, but both had a weathered aura that sighed for a time gone by. The still-s of the evening air amplified the chirping of crickets.

Croaking bullfrogs protested loudly as I made my way to the house with their luggage. Large, white blossoms of a moonflower vine spilled onto the walkway, obscuring the path, but the fragrance of Viva's honeysuckle bushes led me directly to the front door.

Now, I wanted to see Darrell. The kitchen light glowed through the darkness like a beacon leading me safely home. I could not wait for a warm hug, a warm bath, and a night of him cradling me in his arms. As I burst through the door, I could tell by his scowl that the evening would be anything but warm.

"I want you to listen to this," he said as he pushed the play button on the answering machine I used for the *Barber Gazette*.

Deep, gravelly words emanated from the speaker.

"This is Joseph Hacker. Ezra is dead, but the past isn't. Let it go!" The altered voice held a sinister tone.

I felt the blood drain from my face. Darrell sat in silence, awaiting my reaction.

"That can't be your dad. He's dead. It's a prank," I blurted. I wanted to believe it, but in this messed-up journey packed with twists, turns, and lies, I could not be sure.

Darrell fell back in his chair. He knew I had uncovered his family history.

*Oh, why did I say those words?*

His body remained slumped as he stared at the floor, cupping his hands together on his knees. He didn't speak for a long time.

"No good will come of this, Kay," he murmured. "There is more to this story and many who do not want it revealed. This is dangerous. Give it up."

I said nothing. I did not know if I *could* give it up. He

might feel betrayed now, but so did I when I found out about his adoption. Darrell sprinkled the truth with a dust of lies. I prayed morning would break the tension, but right now I wanted a warm bath and a bed.

In the morning, Darrell acted as if nothing had happened. Neither a peep nor a sign of disagreement or concern about the message on the recorder surfaced. I felt relieved, but also a little puzzled. My rigid, self-imposed rules never allowed me to bury conflict and move on. My life always required a resolution, but not today. My weariness begged for peace.

I could not rein in the undercurrent of mistrust running through my mind, however. Did Darrell's actions mean he wanted to protect me or deceive me? I knew in my heart I would never give up my quest. I also understood I would never share this with him.

Darrell, Viva, and, yes, sweet Bessie had grown accustomed to living in the shadows of truth. They shared little and only to get what they wanted. I had to learn to play.

# Chapter IX

I relished my return to the *Gazette*. I parked the Jeep in front of the office and strolled in. Disheveled stacks of papers greeted me. Notes and news requiring transcription littered the desk, and the light on the answering machine blinked as full. Every soul in the county called in to report their social activities of the past week. Now, I had to compile these events into columns, proofing every name so no one would get their feathers ruffled — one misspelling could trigger a never-ending flurry of grousing.

I paid little attention to the content as I hacked away on the computer. I listened to the recorded messages and then turned to the pile of notes people had dropped through the mail slot.

Most of the stack held notes written on the back of small postcards or scribbled on notebook paper and tucked in an envelope. However, one large manila envelope protruded. It had my name in letters cut from a newspaper glued to the front. Inside, a page from a spiral notebook contained a message, also formed with letters cut from a newspaper: "Ezra Hacker is dead, but the past is not. Let it go!" I shivered. The truth about Cowboy cut deep into Ezra's suicide.

By the time I finished, dusk had shrouded the streets of Barber. My anxiety worsened, making the drive home drag on. I pulled in the driveway. The dark house crouched in the shadows like a cat ready to pounce. No lights. No Darrell. *Where in the world was he?* Backing out, I pointed the Jeep toward Viva's house. I didn't want to be alone.

Potholes pocked the narrow dirt road leading to Viva's, forcing me to drive with care. Yet, every ounce of my being screamed: "*floor it.*" Viva only lived four miles from town, but it seemed like an eternity before I caught a glimmer of light from the farmhouse. The old homestead, intimidating in the daytime, turned frightening at night. The drive ended a good distance from the house, so I ran like a madwoman to reach the safety of her porch. Before I could knock, the door opened.

"Come in, dear," Viva said.

She held the door as I entered the living room. It looked different at night. The grass-green carpet, green velour couch, and pale green walls made me feel like a pit in the center of an olive. One minuscule light fixture in the center of the ceiling did not meet the challenge of lighting the entire space, draping the corners in dark shadows.

"Come on in. Bessie and I were just going over some of Ora's papers."

I stared. *She expected me?*

"Where are your things?" she asked.

*My things? Why would I have any "things" with me?*

"Didn't you get Darrell's message?" Her eyebrows rose.

*No. What message?* If Viva read my silence, she did not let on.

"Well, he said he tried to leave a message on that answering machine at the *Gazette*, but it was full or something. So, he left you a note at the house. He said you might stay with me while he's gone. I just figured that's why you showed up."

Okay. I would play.

"I came in a hurry and forgot my things. If you could loan me a gown this evening, I'll head back tomorrow and grab what I need." I had no intention of driving into town this evening.

"Sure," she said. "Now, hurry, dear. Bessie is getting the best of us, and besides, I bet you're hungry. We waited for supper on you." Her eyes flickered with excitement.

*She must be on to something.*

Now, a member of the "Player's Club," I would share nothing of the message and the letter about Ezra Hacker, or express my distrust of Darrell's behavior. I chose to clench my fist of cards until I saw the hand they dealt.

Viva turned and ambled toward the dining room. I followed willingly. The aroma of hot coffee danced with the savory scent of ham and beans bubbling on the stove. Hunger disarmed me. I had not eaten all day. If I ate with two likely fibbers, then so be it.

A genuine smile lit Bessie's face, but her tiny fingers darted quickly to stuff a pile of papers into a box as I entered the room. The box did not belong to Viva. I made a mental note, but I did not have the energy to dissect what it meant. Instead, I plopped into the nearest chair and watched as Viva filled bowls with the savory fare. She dropped an enormous slice of cornbread dripping with melted butter on my plate. The room fell quiet as we busied ourselves with eating. Viva cleared the table and placed a steamy cup of hot coffee in front of me before anyone spoke another word. I felt the knot in my shoulders relaxing. Perhaps my mind made too much of this "Cowboy" saga. *Maybe ...*

Bessie cupped her hand over her mouth as she leaned in close to Viva. "Can we ask her now?" she whispered.

Her expression mimicked that of a southern coquette pleading with a suitor. Viva, on the other hand, seemed perturbed.

"Not yet," she growled.

Viva leaned back and crossed her arms, attempting to put an end to the matter. The knots in my muscles snapped back into place.

"All right, you two. Out with it! You're whispering in front of me like I don't have ears."

Viva surrendered first.

"The time's not right, Kay. But, Bessie can't keep her thoughts to herself." She shot a sideways glance at her friend.

Bessie beamed a demure smile without a trace of contrition.

"We, uh ... well ... we want you to meet Granny Snow," Viva said with some hesitation.

"You want to introduce me to your friend, Granny Snow. That's *it?*"

"Well, not exactly. Don't you know?"

"Why don't you tell me." My annoyance sounded in my words.

"It will wait until morning. We're all tired, and Granny Snow's too important to talk about with your attitude," she snipped right back.

I agreed. My weary bones needed rest. She delivered the promised gown, and I climbed the narrow stairs to the bedroom. The windows sat low to the floor. I lay in bed, watching lightning bugs blink in the dark. Just as I drifted off to sleep a sharp beam of light streaked across the screen. I startled, my eyes wide open. I lay for a long time watching the night sky. No beam of light appeared again. I must have been dreaming. My imagination, that's it. It must be my imagination. I let go of my fears as I welcomed the liberation of sleep.

The bright morning sun streaked through the window. I smelled bacon frying and the strong aroma of fresh coffee, but could not coax myself out of bed. I needed time to process yesterday with a clear mind. For starters, I had received sinister, if not threatening, mail at the office. Then, Darrell left town for an extended period making no real effort to contact me. Last, but not least, Viva wanted me to meet the mysterious Granny Snow. The mail episode would have to wait, but I could go to town and find the elusive note from Darrell. First, though, I would hear Viva out.

I slipped into yesterday's clothes and marched downstairs. Viva and Bessie waited for me to join them. The tension I felt last night had disappeared, so I prepared to listen.

"Now, tell me about Granny Snow. Is she a friend of yours?"

I had never heard of the woman, but no surprise there.

"No," Viva said. "She's not a friend. But, everyone in these parts knows about Granny Snow's pa. Many believe he was Frank James, Jesse's Woodson's brother. Rumors and talk say as much. If he is really Frank James, it would make him Cowboy's uncle. Kay, it's worth a shot."

Viva stirred her coffee with a vengeance. The spoon clink-clanked as she continued her attack on the long-dissolved sugar, her gaze never leaving the swirling black liquid.

I had become familiar with Viva's calculated approach to any topic. She wanted me to open the door, and then she would rush in on the take. Sweet Bessie remained silent, her eyes darting between us. I would do it, but Viva and Bessie needed to stew a minute before I answered.

"Okay, I will meet this Granny Snow. But, right now, I am headed home. I'll see you this evening."

I read the disappointment on both their faces. I agreed too easily, removing the chance for them to coach me on my coming encounter with the infamous Granny Snow. I grabbed my coat and purse and scooted out.

Curious to see if Darrell left a note, I made a beeline for my house. A hastily scrawled note lay partially hidden under other papers on the kitchen table, just as Viva said.

"Kay, sorry I had to leave on such short notice, but there's an emergency at a well site. I'm away for at least two weeks. The location is remote and no phones nearby. Please stay with Mom until I get back. Love, Darrell."

Short, sweet, and equally suspicious, the message did little to put my mind at ease.

I turned my attention to the acquaintance of Granny Snow. I had not asked where I might find this woman, but I refused to have any more conversation about the topic with Viva. In my years of training in science, I knew I did not want to come to a conclusion and select only the elements that supported it. I wanted to find Granny Snow and let her tell me her story without editorial comment from my mother-in-law. The name Snow sounded familiar. I had written a tidbit in last week's column about a family named Snow that lived in the county.

I returned to the *Gazette* and pulled the proof. Skimming the column, I found it. Now, I would call the family. Surely, someone would point me in the right direction.

"Yes," a gruff, female voice answered. Her tone did not

invite conversation.

"This is Kay with the *Barber Gazette*. I am trying to locate Granny Snow," I said.

"What for?"

"Well … I hope to do an article about her father, Frank James." The idea to interview Granny Snow as a reporter fell out of the blue, but seemed like a good approach.

"Wait." The woman sounded harsh.

I sat through the silence, not sure if she had hung up. A lifetime plus one second passed before Granny answered the phone.

"Hello?" she said in an unsure voice.

"Granny, my name is Kay. I am a reporter with the *Barber Gazette*. I want to write a story about your father."

"Missy, I've spent my life talking to reporters about my pa. They all acted interested, pretended to believe me, and then they wrote nothing but garbage. They make it sound like I am crazy or that Pa told lies. I am ninety years old and have little left in me. I'm sorry, but I can't talk to you."

She dressed me down soundly through no fault of my own.

"Granny, please. I am not like those reporters." I sounded weak. I needed something better than that to wheedle in. "I am married to Darrell. His mother was Ora James, Jesse Cole's wife. I want to hear your story, and I'm not out to make you sound crazy. I just want the truth. Your pa might be Jesse Cole's uncle. I need help to piece this together." There, I spilled my guts because I had nothing to lose.

Her silence spoke to her conflict of being ridiculed again or having the chance to share her life with someone who might believe her.

"So, Viva is your mother-in-law?" she asked with an edge.

"Yes," I answered, not sure if I had weakened my plea. Inside my head, I counted 1-2-3-4-5 …

"Missy, I will meet you once. Just once. I live with my son, and he won't like this. Come tomorrow afternoon and come alone. I don't want a lot of fuss."

"Okay. See you tomorrow." I had done it. I got an interview with Granny Snow.

I returned to Viva's for the evening. She and Bessie met me at the door.

"Did you find her? Will she talk to you?" Viva uttered as I walked in.

"Nothing," I replied. I did not want to share anything until I knew more. "I'll try again tomorrow."

Their faces drooped with disappointment.

"Just to let you know, dear, it won't be easy to get Granny to meet you. Viva and I tried a few weeks ago. Her son had a conniption. You'd have thought we were askin' to see the President. I have never been treated so rudely and …" Bessie's voice trailed off.

I looked up just in time to catch Viva giving her the evil eye. Viva and Bessie had been busy. When they failed, Viva sent me in as reinforcements. Glad I held my tongue.

# Chapter X

I spent the morning writing down every question I could think of for Granny. After all, I only had one chance. I put my papers and notebook in the Jeep and headed to Barber. I stopped at an Exxon station on the edge of town to get gas and directions. A tall, skinny kid with a ball cap and an oil smudged shirt approached the Jeep.

"I need to fill up, and … could you tell me how to get to Granny Snow's house?"

"The gas is easy, but Granny's is a different story." He flashed a full-faced grin. "Just get on Farm Road 273 and go three miles. Then turn left onto a gravel road."

"Wait," I said. "Would you write it down for me, please? I will never remember."

"Yes, ma'am." He sketched on the paper I handed him. "The road is rough. That Jeep of yours will come in handy."

The boy handed me the map he had drawn. As he walked away, he slapped the rear of the Jeep like a jockey sending a horse off to race.

The road morphed from asphalt to gravel shortly after I left town. I blessed my four-wheel drive for the thousandth time as I bumped over the washboard gravel road leading to Granny's house. Granny lived at the edge of the county, and all back roads in Arkansas were rough and narrow. Soon after I made the last turn, I spied the whitewashed farmhouse sitting at the top of the knoll. The vintage shotgun-style house sat proudly at the top, like a sentinel in the noonday sun. I parked at the edge of the road and climbed the steep hill. Brown grass, burned crisp by summer heat, crunched under my feet. I kept my eyes on the ground, mindful of copperhead snakes, as I marched toward the house with a steady and deliberate step that belied my apprehension. When I glanced up, a large man in bib overalls and a small, thin woman stood on the porch. We stared at each other for a moment. I waited for an invitation inside. Surely, I found the right house.

"Come in," the man said flatly. The woman did not speak at all.

"Thank you." I made my way to the steps. The man looked familiar. He reminded me of Skeeter.

I followed the man through the hallway until we reached a room at the back. It looked like a porch converted into a bedroom. Windows lined two sides, offering a panoramic view of the bluffs and canyons that stretched for miles. Sunlight illuminated the room filled with pictures, books, and papers stacked neatly around the edges. A mere slip of a woman sat at a small table in the corner. High cheekbones accentuated the hollows of her cheeks and the depth of her eyes. Time had withered her face but had failed to steal her beauty.

"Have a seat, missy," she said, patting the chair next to her. I took the designated seat without a word. I had no time to waste.

"I appreciate you meeting with me. I have so many questions, and I hope you have some answers." Nothing like groveling, but I meant it.

"I have some questions too, missy. Age before beauty." Granny laughed aloud, amused by her own wit.

I'm sure she wanted to know about me and why I had come. I would answer honestly, but, in truth, I did not know the answers myself.

"First, tell me about you and Darrell."

"Of course. What do you want to know?"

"When and where did you meet?"

"Well, Darrell and I met through a mutual friend while I was teaching at the university. You might call it a whirlwind courtship. We dated for two months and got married two years ago. Then we moved back to Barber last year to help Viva."

"Did you know Kendra, Darrell's first wife?" she asked.

This question made me uncomfortable. Darrell never spoke of her. Viva adored her, and I fought that jealousy daily.

"No," I answered, plain and true.

"I didn't think so," she replied. "What about Darrell? Did you know he was Ora's grandson? That Jesse Cole was his grandpa by marriage?"

"Yes," I said matter-of-factly. I wondered if Granny could see through my half-truth.

"Did Darrell tell you?"

She knew.

"No," I mumbled, ashamed to admit it.

"Do you trust Darrell? Do you trust Viva?" Granny machine-gunned the questions at me, hoping to hit a target, and she did.

This woman peeled away the layers of my heart. If I chose the truth, I would betray my family. If I chose a lie, she would know. She knew Viva and Darrell better than I did. What else did she know?

"Not completely."

"Sorry, missy," she said. "This is the only way to test your nerve."

"Why on earth do you need to test my nerve? Do you think I came to harm you?"

Granny's eyes narrowed. "There are those out to harm me. What's more, if I tell you my story, they will be out to harm you, too. I can't trust a liar or a weakling with my secrets. You seem to be neither."

I nodded. The faint of heart would not survive this journey. Darrell and Viva had warned of the danger, but it never seemed real. Now, I had to decide if I was strong enough to know the truth or call it off and retreat. I guess I made that decision when I took the stone from the Rosebud plantation. I must know the truth.

"Then, you trust me? You don't think I am weak?"

She shook her head slowly. "Missy, you can tell a lot about a person through their eyes. Not only do you look at people, your eyes cut right through them. Lies go in one pile and truth in another. Most liars or just plain stupid people would be afraid to face you head-on. I like that in a person. You've got a level head on your shoulders, and you don't lack for smarts."

Granny had dissected my soul in minutes. I never tolerated stupidity or lies. Her sharp analysis after such a short visit surprised me.

"How can you know all of this? We just met."

"I met you a long time ago, Kay. I just never saw you in person. I allowed you to come so I could get a read on you. We are a lot alike, missy," she answered. "But, beware of Darrell. You're a little blind about that husband of yours. I bet he avoids looking you in the eye."

I flinched inside. Darrell had seemed evasive of late and frequently dropped his gaze in our conversations about Cowboy. I would worry about that later. I needed to focus on the task at hand.

"This is my only chance to find out what I need to know. Is it my turn now?" I asked.

Granny chuckled. "You only got one chance *if* you had lied to me. Or worse yet, lied to yourself. You did neither."

"Then, let's get started," I said. "I want to know all about your pa ... Frank James."

# Chapter XI

An occasional breeze blew through the windows but provided little relief from the stifling heat. Granny shuffled over to a well-worn rocker closer to the window and sat down, pulling the skirt of her dress above her knees. Now, she seemed ready.

"I grew up right here in Newton County in a little shack just over yonder. Ma, Pa, and eleven of us kids. Lordy, can you imagine thirteen of us living in a tiny cabin?" she said as she kicked back with a laugh.

Thirteen people living in a two-bedroom shack sounded like a nightmare. No indoor plumbing, no air conditioning, and no running water existed back then. Thank you, no.

"Never had much company except late at night," Granny said, her drawl more pronounced as her mind drifted back. "Three men came by at least once a month to see Pa. Each time, Ma herded all of us kids to the bedroom, closing the door behind her. I caught sight of a face sometimes, but I only knew one of them. They stayed long into the night and mostly talked in whispers, but sometimes one or the other got riled up, and I heard pieces of what they said. I can't remember all of it, but I do remember they called Pa, Frank. Folks around here knew Pa as Joe … Joe Vaughn. As a child, I didn't let it worry me none. I know what that means now, for sure."

Granny stopped talking, letting the impact of her words sink in.

"Go on," I said. Like with Viva and Bessie, I had to pull details out of her like a dentist extracting a tooth. "Who were these night strangers?"

"I'm getting to that part, girl," she scolded. "Pa did some farming, but mostly, he surveyed for Newton County." Granny Snow rocked back and forth in the squeaky old chair as she shared her story. "Sometimes, he would just get up and leave in the middle of the night. He would be gone a week at a time, traipsing in those woods, leaving Ma to wrestle us kids. He always left a note on her pillow before leaving. Even so, Ma sure got cranky when he took off like that."

*Hmmm … this sounded a lot like Darrell. Our men preferred their freedom and thought a note pacified their wives. Interesting.*

"At fifteen, I married Charlie, and we moved two counties over. I didn't come around much until Pa lay on his deathbed. By that time, Ma had passed, and the kids had scattered … it fell on me to care for him." Her bony hands clenched the arms of the rocker as if their abandonment still stirred up anger. "Many a night I sat with Pa. He rambled on and on about his life. I think most dying men do. Then he said something really strange. He told me when he died he wanted his real name on the tombstone. I asked what name that would be. Pa said he wanted 'Frank James' on his marker." Her words flowed easily as if she had told the story many times.

"So, out of the blue, your pa announced he was Frank James?"

Granny scrunched her eyes and scowled. "I never knew Pa to be a liar. If he said he was Frank James, then he was Frank James. End of story."

*Be subtle*, I reminded myself. No need to waste the trip by getting tossed out on my ear.

"Like I said, I spent a lot of time with Pa at the end. Pa told me he and his brother Jesse fought with Quantrill during the Civil War. When the war ended, Pa settled in Indian Territory. That's Oklahoma now," she added. "When he moved on, he left everything behind — his family, his past, and his name — and settled in the Ozarks.

"So, when his time came, I did as he asked. Pa's headstone reads 'Frank James.'" The stringent words dared me to cross her.

I met the challenge. My gaze never wavered. I locked my thoughts deep inside. One ounce of disbelief or doubt would finish me.

Now, I knew the story of the Newton County Frank James, but I had gained nothing on Cowboy. Surely, Viva had not sent me here for this.

"Go home."

A deep, stern voice startled me. The man resembling Skeeter stood in the doorway, motioning for me to leave.

I opened my mouth to protest, but his set jaw and crossed arms left little room for interpretation. Granny's stoic expression offered no clue to her feelings about his demand. I gathered my notebook and scurried to the door, murmuring thank you to Granny as I left. Little came from the visit. No questions answered. No questions raised. Back in my Jeep, I headed to Viva's.

My tires kicked up dust, fogging the road. The afternoon sun sunk lower in the sky, but the heat did not relent. A glistening stream on the right side beckoned to me. I wanted nothing more than to dangle my feet in the cool, rippling water and contemplate, once again, on this journey I called my life. I pulled over and parked under a county sign marking Race Horse Creek.

Craggy stones and boulders lined the bank, making my descent difficult. I picked my way down the slope, watching for snakes or other critters that might hide in the crevices. A large, flat boulder about thirty feet down looked like the perfect resting spot. As I drew closer, I saw strange markings etched in the hard rock; etchings similar to ones on the rock in my Jeep. My mind reflected on Viva's words when I had shown her the rock from Rosebud Bend.

"Sentinels, as we called them, guarded our stashes, waiting for the day the South would rise again. They marked the locations with the secret codes of the Knights of the Golden Circle carved into stones. That's what you found today. The mark of a sentinel for the KGC."

*Mercy me. This boulder must be a part of Cowboy's puzzle.*
The sun had completely disappeared behind the hills, plunging the valley into darkness. I scurried up the bank, clutched by an unknown fear. I had always been afraid of the dark, but visions of sentinels and secret codes added new dimensions to my anxiety. I jumped into my Jeep and headed to Viva's. Disappointment and excitement competed with my emotions as I slowly made my way back. I needed to know more from Granny, but I may never have another chance. On the other hand, I had found a matching stone, one that could be very

important in my search for the truth about Cowboy.

Viva and Bessie did not quiz me upon my return. *Why should they?* I never told them I had a meeting with Granny Snow. The next few days dragged on with work at the *Gazette* and long evenings at the farmhouse. Bessie and Viva picked through their piles of Cowboy's memorabilia without as much as a word to me. I quietly pretended to read.

Darrell would be home in about a week. I wanted to see him, but he had hurt my feelings when he left with just a note. I felt as if I didn't have a friend in the world, but I needed to get over it. Truthfully, Granny had brought my misgivings about Viva and Darrell front and center. I felt disloyal. This journey put a wedge between me and the only family and friends I had. I still faced the windowpane, only this time, I sat on the inside looking out. I had to find the answer to Cowboy's mystery so life could get back on track.

The next morning, I received a phone call at the *Gazette*. "Granny wants to see you this afternoon. Come alone and tell no one," the voice of the woman who stood on Granny's porch the other day commanded me. Her tone didn't matter. I intended to keep the appointment.

The drive seemed much shorter this time. The large man and the spindly woman greeted me like before. I followed the man down the hall and took my designated seat near the window.

"Hello, missy," Granny said.

"Hello, Granny. I wasn't sure if I would ever see you again." I hoped to sound lighthearted, but I could not have been more serious.

"You're not a treasure hunter, are you, girl?" She arched her eyebrows.

The question sounded like a statement.

"Not really, unless you call looking for the truth about Cowboy a treasure hunt." Her words agitated me, but I knew better than to say so.

"I think it's safe to continue. The story I told about Pa is no secret. Lord knows every reporter within a hundred miles came to hear about him. But, they thought I was crazy. You're different. My gut tells me you know how to keep your mouth shut." She shook a bony finger in my direction to emphasize her words.

Today, Granny seemed smaller, a little frailer. I reminded myself that she was ninety years old, even though her spunk denied the years. She had a story to tell, and, like me, she lacked trusted confidants. For whatever reason, she had selected me.

"I'm old, and the story is long. It must live on after me, but I don't want it in the wrong hands. You'll understand when I am done." Moments passed in silence as Granny stared out the window at the tall poplars rustling gently in the wind.

"You know the Cheyenne people used to pass along their secrets to a tribal leader to keep the history and beliefs of the culture alive. They charged him with their most sacred possession: their culture and stories. They called him *Keeper of the Arrows*. Will you be the *Keeper of the Arrows* for me?"

"Yes," I promised. I could not answer any other way. I just prayed I would live up to my word. I had made so many promises lately, but somehow, they were one and the same. First Viva, then Bessie, and now Granny vested secrets of the James family with me. These three elderly women extracted promises, though deep down, I knew each wanted more than the safekeeping of stories. *But, what?* Only time would tell.

"Let me tell you about Jesse, or Cowboy, as you call him. Jesse Cole had a very curious personality. I'm not sure if you could believe all he told you. He always talked in riddles," she said.

I knew Cowboy talked in riddles, but I also knew that truth lined every word he spoke. Perhaps in time, I would share this with Granny, but not now.

"If he just told the truth, he would be interesting enough. Charlie, my husband, told me that once when he was walking home as a boy, he heard shooting. He saw a wagon with a still in the back barreling down the road toward him. It rattled and shook and made lots of banging noises. The driver kept looking over his shoulder, the law not far behind. Guess they raided that still, and Cowboy just happened to be there. It seems he felt a duty to defend the still. And, mind you, it didn't even belong to him." Granny's lips curved in a wide grin as she reveled in the irony of it all.

"The sheriff got a shot off at Cowboy. Thought he had killed him. But, as soon as the sheriff walked over to see the body, Cowboy raised up his gun and sent a bullet plum through the sheriff's hat. Let me tell you, the sheriff and his men fired everything they had at Cowboy and left him for dead." She paused, for my benefit or her amusement, I couldn't say.

"Well, Cowboy managed his way to the Jewell house — David Jewell was a doctor. They took Cowboy to a hospital in either Sugar Grove or Booneville, not sure which. He pulled through, and guess what?"

I shrugged. These meandering anecdotes drove me crazy, but I couldn't shake the old woman and scream, "Get on with it."

"As soon as he got out of the hospital, they made him a

deputy sheriff!" She licked her lips with relish, remembering his brush with the law.

"Cowboy never would tell whose still it was, though," she added with a wink.

"So, the men who tried to kill Cowboy made him a sheriff?" I asked.

"Not exactly. The men that tried to kill him disappeared. We never saw them again. That was the last time the local guys ever made a raid. After that, the feds took over. Cleaned house and the local sheriff vanished."

*Amazing*, I thought. Who pulled strings to make that happen? Undercurrents flowed through Cowboy's story. I wanted to ask questions, but Granny picked right back up again.

"Missy, there's something else you need to understand. Life was hard. Making a living, tough. The mountain people here made whiskey; the ones in the valley farmed. Anyway, good people made moonshine to survive. My cousin later told me the still belonged to Otto, Orinda's husband — you know, Ora's sister. I never would have thought Otto had a still. I think it may have belonged to his family. Anyhow, Otto's dad was the mayor of Barber. Otto did a short term in prison for running whiskey."

I got it. Jesse Cole came to the aid of his brother-in-law, and Otto's father rewarded him for it.

"Political allies must be a great asset in these Arkansas hills," I muttered snidely.

"Missy, you're not listening? Do you really think Otto's pa sent him to prison and made Jesse Cole a sheriff?"

My brain must have shut off. No one would let their son go to prison and promote some in-law to sheriff. If politics played a part, Otto's father did not call the shots.

"Otto was one of the nicest, mildest people I had ever known. Hard to picture him as a bootlegger running from the law. He had outrun them before. But, this time, Orinda went with him, and he wouldn't run. Maybe he worried she'd get hurt. Anyway, the pen broke his spirit. When he got out, he quit the moonshining business. Never heard what happened to him after that."

Old people share too much information. Granny assumed I knew these people and their lives. I did not. However, I gained an understanding of Cowboy through Otto's plight. Some sense of loyalty must have run through his veins if he risked his life for Otto's still.

The room felt like a furnace in the midday heat. I needed fresh air and a cool drink, but I did not want to lose any time collecting details.

"Granny, are you up for a short trip into town? Would you like ice cream or perhaps a soda?" I asked.

"That would hit the spot, missy."

"Let's go then."

I grabbed my notebook and briefcase, took Granny's hand, and headed down the hall. The large man from the porch made his presence known but did not stop our exit. He and Granny exchanged glances as we passed. I felt his suspicions about my motives, yet he deferred his judgment to that of his mother's.

I cranked the air conditioner up in the Jeep, hoping to cool it down quickly. If the heat worked hard on me, it must have been worse for Granny. She fanned herself with a handkerchief she found in her worn black purse. The gentle fanning motion slowed and then stopped altogether as the temperature in the Jeep became tolerable.

"Please tell me more," I said as I navigated the winding dirt road.

"Well, at my age, my mind doesn't travel in a straight line. I kind of jump around from story to story. I remember a lot, just not in the right order. But, you're young enough to rearrange and make sense of my babblings," she said chuckling. Her apologetic tone betrayed her merry laugh.

"When Cowboy first came to Barber, he was all shot up and half-dead in the back of a boxcar."

Ah, I knew the boxcar story as Viva had told it. Maybe the circle would start to close. I turned the blower down so I could hear every word.

"Where did he come from?" I tried not to sound too anxious, but I needed to connect some dots.

"Where did he come from?" she repeated. "Well, I know Cowboy was the son of Jesse Woodson James and an Emma Anders or Andrews. I'm not sure which."

The story began to converge. I squashed my excitement, so Granny would keep talking.

"Jesse Woodson stayed around Marlin in Falls County, Texas, going by the name of Jesse Redmond. Quite the charmer, I hear. Anyway, he took up with a young girl by the name of Emma Anders. Emma came from a good family. Her sister, Ida, was the toast of the town. When Emma became pregnant with Jesse Cole, the Anders household had no room for an unmarried girl with a bastard child. Why she was only a child herself. Well, anyway ... I think the James family in Houston County, Texas, took her in."

Eureka! The affidavit that Viva kept in the box came from Houston County. Viva and Granny had matching stories.

Granny enjoyed our outing. Chocolate dip cones from the Dairy Boy provided just the ticket to cool down a hot summer afternoon. The steady blast from the air conditioner took its toll on the tall swirl of ice cream, however. Tiny drops slid under the edge of the cone and dripped steadily in Granny's lap. Her cheeks turned pink as she struggled.

"I eat like a baby," she said with dismay.

She fumbled in her purse and yanked out a wad of tissue to clean up the mess. A yellowed piece of paper fell onto the car seat. It looked like a map with strange drawings and symbols similar to the ones on the sentinel rocks. Granny snatched the ragged paper, shoving it back into her bag.

We pretended it did not happen.

I chose, instead, to make small talk as we drove. Granny shifted gears just as easily. We chatted incessantly and talked of nothing.

As the Jeep approached Race Horse Creek, I pulled off the road. I wanted to see Granny's reaction to the markings on the flat sandstone rock, the markings that matched the map she had stuffed in her purse.

"Granny, this creek is just beautiful. Makes you want to dangle your feet in that cool water, doesn't it?"

She stared out her window.

"I'll just be a minute." I reached for the door.

"No," she said in a voice much too loud. "Take me home. I need to go home."

The panic in her voice sounded real.

"Okay, another time," I said.

I had learned what I needed to know. The resemblance of the stones to the map extended beyond coincidence, and this creek harbored clues. I would return to Race Horse Creek alone.

During the rest of the trip, Granny fidgeted with her dress, smoothing imaginary wrinkles with weathered hands. I felt a pang of guilt for upsetting this elderly lady, but not enough guilt to regret what I had done. If I am to be the *Keeper of the Arrows*, she must unlock the secrets tucked away in her heart. I hoped I had not scared her away.

Only a few days remained before Darrell's return. I needed to make the most of them. He disapproved of my doings with Viva, so I could just imagine his anger now that Granny Snow joined my circle of collaborators. She cast a heap of doubt on my relationship with Darrell. I did not completely trust him: perhaps because he did not tell me Viva adopted him, perhaps because of his reaction to Cowboy, perhaps because I did not really know him at all.

Darrell and I met at the university's annual year-end faculty party. I huddled in a corner talking theory with my peers when I noticed a middle-aged man shadowing my department supervisor, Mark, as he made his way around the room. He stood slightly less than six feet. His silvery-blond hair a sharp contrast to his sun-weathered complexion. His shirt, the color of a hard blue sky, accentuated the blue in his eyes. I could not ignore his presence. This man smiled and talked with each encounter, but an air of aloofness hovered about him like a cloud. I avoided social events like the plague and had no desire to make new acquaintances, except one. I wanted to meet this man.

"And, here she is," said Mark, "the one and only Kay Davenport." He turned to me. "I mentioned your research to Darrell. I hope you don't mind. He is doing some research as well. I think it's in Rocks and Clods."

Darrell grimaced as Mark howled. He apparently did not appreciate the denigrating label for geology. I sensed Darrell disliked this environment as much as I did. On impulse, I grabbed his hand.

"Let's go for a walk. I'd like to hear about your work."

Relief spread across his face. We spent a relaxing afternoon strolling around campus, but never once did our work enter the conversation. From that time on, I wanted to spend every spare moment with Darrell. With him, I felt a release from a lifetime of work and loneliness. I was ready for a change, and Darrell provided the catalyst.

In hindsight, I did not really know my husband. I only knew the present tense of his life, not the past. I feared that circumstance would haunt me.

# Chapter XII

Viva and Bessie startled as I opened the door. Bessie dropped her needlework on her lap, and Viva scrambled to put Ora's papers away.

"Come on in and sit down, Kay. It's hotter than a firecracker out there," Viva said with fake casualness.

I did as suggested. The cool, damp air of a swamp cooler provided relief from the sweltering heat of Arkansas in August. Viva brought me a tumbler of icy-cold sweet tea as I settled myself into the large green recliner. I welcomed this oasis.

The afternoon grew late. I finally decided to share my visits to Granny's with Viva and Bessie — or at least part of them. They had wanted more from her than Cowboy's story. Tonight, I would try to find the answer.

"I met Granny Snow today," I announced. I had told the truth – just not the whole truth.

"Tell, do tell," Bessie said. It sounded like a line from *Gone with the Wind*. Dear Bessie could not help but be charming.

The winds had shifted. Tonight, I controlled the discussion. They had no idea what I had learned. I would test their mettle.

"Get comfortable, ladies. We have a lot of talking to do."

Viva raised a finger in the air. "Okay, just give me a minute while I get this hair off my neck." She had taken my order to get comfortable seriously.

Bessie pulled a chair close to the swamp cooler to prepare for our chat. Soon, Viva emerged from the bedroom, tucking her wispy locks into a hairnet. *Showtime.*

Viva had told me about the sentinels at Rosebud, and Granny Snow carried a map. These two threads connected. I needed to find out how. I knew enough from Granny to bait. Time to see what I could catch.

"Was Cowboy a sentinel?"

I hit it straight on. Viva had once described Cowboy as a sentinel, but I needed to know exactly what she meant. I hoped they would believe Granny had shared it with me. Viva's lips parted as if to respond, but she said nothing. Bessie, on the other hand, bobbed her head up and down in affirmation.

"How do you know that for sure?" I asked. "I know Granny's story, so now I want to hear yours," I added for reinforcement. Dusting words with lies became a newfound art.

Viva bit first.

"Well, Cowboy didn't just come out of the blue, don't you know? He rode a boxcar into town, all shot up, and … "

"Yes, Viva, I know the story of the boxcar," I interrupted.

"What did Granny tell you?" she countered.

Actually, Viva had told me this part herself. Apparently, she did not remember.

"She told me plenty, but I want to know how you *knew*

Cowboy was a sentinel."

"Ora," she stated.

"Ora told you?" I asked. This didn't seem likely.

"Not exactly." She shrugged. "But, sort of. Ora didn't talk much about it at first. Later, she told me she was afraid because of what had happened to Ezra. That poem ate at her like lye on ash. Sometimes she asked me, 'How could I cause it all?' and then other times she'd say, 'I'm the reason Ezra's dead.' Back and forth she went, driving herself crazy. Driving me crazy, too, for sure."

It must have pained Viva to watch her friend torment herself. Losing a loved one crushes your soul. And, if you feel responsible for it, the agony is unbearable.

"After a time, Ora started telling me bits and pieces."

I raised an eyebrow and leaned back in the recliner. "I want to know all the bits and pieces, as you call them."

Viva sighed. She could tell my patience wore thin.

"Well, it started when Ora and Cowboy bought eighty acres and built a house. Now, mind you, no one had any money back then. No one. My husband worked on the river. We got by, but most folks farmed or ran moonshine just to eat. Not Ora and Cowboy. They seemed to have plenty, while the rest of us lived hand-to-mouth. So, I just asked her where on earth that money came from. You know what she told me?"

Viva paused, waiting for me to ask. I remained silent. She pouted a moment and then continued.

"She told me when Cowboy disappeared for short periods, a Cherokee man appeared at the edge of the woods. No matter what the weather, rain or shine, he stood guard and waited until Cowboy came home. They talked for a while, and Cowboy would take off again the next day. He would leave her a note saying he would be back. And, he always returned — with money."

Viva removed her glasses and rubbed her eyes with the tips of her fingers.

"Ora wouldn't say anymore. That was all she knew, and it was good enough for her."

*Yes, Cowboy could keep a secret for sure — and his past was a big one*, I said to myself. The more I heard about him, the more I believed he got tangled up with something much bigger. When Cowboy came to Barber in the middle of the night, he was probably running from the law. On the other hand, he was the law. Another puzzle.

My bait worked. Viva loved to talk about Cowboy. I wondered why Granny didn't trust her or Darrell. I nudged her in a different direction.

"Granny does not seem to trust you and Darrell." My flat tone didn't reveal how my curiosity raged.

"You have no business talking about my son — your husband — with that woman!" Her voice cracked with anger.

"You're the one who wanted me to meet her," I shot back.

"Not to tear my family apart. I wanted you to find out about Cowboy." She scowled. "You're just like Kendra."

Viva stormed off to her bedroom, slamming the door behind her. Her violent reaction took me off guard, and her words cut to the bone. I never wanted to tear my family apart. Nonetheless, I seemed to do so with little effort.

I destroyed my chance with Viva with one sentence. A blanket of loneliness weighed on my body like a shroud. *Why, why, why did I begin this journey?*

Darkness set in. The day had faded as fast as my hopes. The staccato chirp of cicadas accompanied by the tick of the mantle clock magnified the silence of the night as I sat alone in the darkness.

"Come with me, dear. You've stewed long enough."

Bessie placed her hand gently on my forearm and led me to my bedroom.

"I'll be back in a minute," she said.

As promised, Bessie returned lugging a box embossed with roses and ivy, the same box she had hidden under her chair when I had walked into the dining room a few days ago. With care, she untied a black silk ribbon that secured the box, revealing hundreds of letters.

"These will tell you everything you need to know. I love Viva like a sister, but sometimes she's just wrong. She had no reason to fly off the handle like that. She's different from the way she used to be."

She removed the stacks, placing them in rows upon the bed.

"Let's start at the beginning," she said as she opened the oldest of her letters and read.

Dear Bessie,

Hope all is well with you. Thank you for taking the trouble to write after Bud died. You know, I can't believe he's gone. I just ramble around this old house, thinking about Bud and cursing God for taking him from me. He was a good man. Can't see much reason to keep living, but I don't have a choice either, do I?

Didn't mean to burden you with my troubles, but I've no one else to tell. Ora comes by some, but, Lordy, one minute she is blubbering about Ezra and the next she wants to turn on the radio to listen to one of those preachers always asking you to send money. And, she does. Sends them a dollar every week. I'm not sure a dollar is enough to cover her and Cowboy both.

Didn't have much to say. Just wanted to thank you for thinking of me.

Write when you can.

Your friend,
Viva

"Wait a minute," I said. "I thought you hadn't met Viva until we came to Marlin. Bud passed away in 1959 – over thirty years ago."

Bessie nodded. "I know that's what Viva told you. In truth, we've been friends since we were kids. She moved to Barber when she was nine."

"Why would she lie to me?"

"Viva doesn't see it as lying, dear." Bessie's voice had a pleading quality as if asking for forgiveness on Viva's behalf. "She just has a funny way with the truth. She cuts out the pieces she doesn't want to share. It started when Darrell reached his teens. Not sure if she started lying to protect him or herself. I think she got so wrapped up in Darrell and his antics that she just picked what she could deal with in life and let the rest go."

"So, Viva is from Marlin?"

"Yes."

"And, did she know Cowboy?"

"She knew his people … the James family from Plainview over in Houston County."

This would be a long night, but I wanted Bessie to continue the story. Viva would be up in the morning, and the curtain on the truth would drop again.

"Please go on, Bessie. I want to know everything."

"Well, dear, I'll just read the ones about Cowboy. There are a lot of letters here."

"No! Skip nothing." I trusted no one to tell the whole truth. Not even Bessie. I would decide which details held importance.

Bessie read letter after letter, detailing intimate conversations between old friends. A Viva I had never met began to emerge. A widow at forty and childless, she had to fend for herself. She found a job cleaning at a local motel. Each morning she walked five miles to town, worked for eight hours, and then walked back home. This repetitive chain of survival filled her waking hours. Time must have seemed endless to this grieving woman. However, the string of sorrow broke when she adopted Darrell. Words of despair gave way to joy as Viva filled letters with stories of little Darrell. With one small twist of fate, a childless widow had become a doting mother.

I shifted my attention, once again, to Bessie and the letters.

Dear Bessie,

I went to St. Joe yesterday to take the old cow to the vet. It's really rugged down there. The vet said he had to go to a remote cabin out in the hills near here (we still have our hill people). He said he went to check on a sick cow

— the road ended, and he drove down a kind of trail to get there. When he reached the cabin, an old lady came out to meet him. Another old lady was hanging clothes on the line. She told him that was her mother. As best he could figure, she was 102. My friend, Beverly, said she ran a call on that cabin some time ago. The oldest lady had lived in a cave with her family for a while before they built a cabin. Let me tell you, these hills were dangerous during the War and for several years afterward. It was pretty well lawless. Still is, I think. Not much different from Barber.

No, they've got nothing on Barber. You know that Granny Snow I told you about? Her people are hill people. So are Ora and Cowboy. He still goes to town in a buckboard wagon. Now, that's a sight to see. Loads all those kids up in the back, puts a shotgun across his lap, and off they go.

Lots of rough and rugged people still roam these hills. I am afraid Darrell will be just like them.

Well, I have rambled enough for one day. Got canning to do. Write when you get a chance.

Viva

I knew it. Viva had known Granny Snow for a long time. The mantle clock in the living room chimed twice. Bessie and I had been reading for hours. She arched her back and stretched her arms above her head like a cat rising from a nap. Our bodies ached for a good night's rest.

"Calf rope," Bessie said with a giggle.

This time I agreed. Like it or not, we had to continue another time.

"Tomorrow?" I asked as Bessie departed.

Yet, sleep eluded me. Why had Viva said I was like Kendra? Whatever the reason, it did not sound like a compliment. Tomorrow, I would go back to see Granny. I needed to get out of Viva's house but had no desire to go home. Darrell would not return for a few days, and Bessie and I had unfinished business. Granny would provide a good retreat. If she would see me.

# Chapter XIII

The next morning, I rose earlier than usual to avoid Viva. Her reference to Kendra still bothered me. I opened the door at the bottom of the stairs and almost knocked Bessie over.

"What are you doing?" I asked, perturbed by her presence.

"I'm going with you today."

I raised an eyebrow. "Where's Viva?"

"She got up at the crack of dawn. I heard her bustling around the kitchen. A noise woke me up. By the time I got out of bed, she had left."

"Where did she go at this time of day?"

"Don't let it trouble you." She looked me up and down as if she were my mother eyeballing what I wore for my first date. "I guess I could ask you the same thing, dear. Where are you going?"

Bessie had avoided my question and trapped me. I could not see Granny with her in tow. I had no choice but to lie. Lies seemed to come easier now.

"Just for a drive to clear my head," I muttered, still annoyed.

"I thought so," she said with little conviction. "Let's get started."

Bessie wore her customary wide-brimmed, white straw hat and sunglasses, but her jeans and sneakers contrasted with her pale-pink, ruffled blouse. What a sight! Southern charm and Arkansas practicality rolled into a hundred-pound package. She tucked her brocade box of treasures under her arm, grabbed her purse, and stood ready for departure. Clearly, Bessie was not going with me today. I was going with her.

We climbed into the Jeep and headed to town. The first order of business — bacon and eggs with a hot cup of coffee. Surely, Bessie woke up hungry too. I loved to stop at the Pollyanna for breakfast. The Pollyanna had been in business since the forties. Many regulars who preferred to eat in peace sat at one of the bar stools lining a long, gray, Formica counter. Well-worn booths accommodated the ones that wished to mix their meal with gossip. The back booth suited me fine. I had no gossip to share this morning.

Bessie gawked around the room like a bird on a perch, saying little. An occasional sip of coffee or bite of toast interrupted her perusal. I, on the other hand, ate ravenously. Late nights and confrontation had whetted my appetite.

She leaned across the table and whispered, "Look at the people in the very first booth, but don't make it obvious."

I wanted to laugh. I had not spied on people in restaurants since junior high. I turned as nonchalantly as I could. The front, semi-circle booth held several patrons, including Skeeter, who I had not seen since the demolition of the jail. Most seemed like local farmers dressed for a day's work. One, however, looked distinctly different. A clean-cut gentleman in a tan shirt and dark tie anchored the cluster of untidy men. Was this who Bessie wanted me to notice?

"Quit staring," she hissed. "They'll see you."

"Let's go." Her words irritated me. Bessie loved drama, but I was in no mood for such nonsense.

Once in the Jeep, I turned to her. "What was that all about?"

"Did you see the man in the tie? He comes by a lot to see Darrell. I think he's Darrell's friend."

"So?"

Bessie cocked her head to one side, her brows knitted as she studied my face.

"Nothing at all, dear. Just thought you might want to know."

*Why do these old women leave their thoughts dangling? Do they revel in tantalizing a newbie like me?*

"Kay, I hoped we could visit Glendale Baptist Cemetery if we have time."

I had no other plans, but a cemetery seemed an odd choice for an outing.

"Direct the way," I mumbled.

We headed on Route 10 west toward Booneville.

"Turn there," Bessie cried as we passed the farm-to-market road 768.

I slammed on my brakes, too late to make the turn. I backed up and tried again.

"Jeez! I need more warning than that."

"Drive a little slower, dear," she said, patting my shoulder.

I had no choice but to slow down. The newly-graveled road kept slinging pieces of chat at my truck no matter what the speed. Soon, we came to a rounded knoll, heavily shaded by tall pines. A two-rut road threaded through the trees, leading to ornate, wrought-iron gates that guarded the rows of headstones honoring the dead. Bessie stepped out and made her way through the sacred markers. She knew exactly where she wanted to go. I followed her lead but remained a few steps behind. Bessie stopped over the rise near a rectangular slab of marble resting on a well-manicured grave.

"This is Cowboy's grave. I wanted you to see it."

The grave appeared unremarkable except for two things. The inscription read, "Daddy – Jesse Cole James." Such a term of endearment, an expression of affection, seemed odd. Viva led me to believe Cowboy was an unlovable creature, tolerated by those who needed him. The tombstone contradicted her opinion. However, the incongruities in Viva's stories no longer surprised me; they had become just another layer that you must remove to get to the truth about this man.

The second anomaly intrigued me more. Coins and small trinkets lined the top of the headstone. Could these be tokens of tribute? If so, what did they mean?

"Bessie, what are these?"

"Don't touch," she commanded. By now, I had grown accustomed to Bessie's reprimands.

I tucked my hands in my pockets. "All right, but what do they mean?"

"The coins are to show respect for a fallen soldier. Pennies mean you visited the grave and wish to show respect. A nickel means you trained with the soldier. A dime means you served in some capacity with him, and a quarter means you were with him when he was killed."

"Is this a Confederate tradition?"

"No, Kay. I think it started with the Vietnam War, but now many people use it to honor the dead no matter which war they fought in."

Bessie never ceased to amaze me with her knowledge of history.

"And, the trinkets? Why the toy turtles, guns, and other toys?"

"These are special … very special, dear." Bessie cast a wistful glance at the grave. "People place them there to honor Cowboy's life."

The pennies numbered in the hundreds, with approximately a dozen dimes scattered about. But, no one had left a nickel or quarter for Cowboy. By Bessie's account, Cowboy, a well-respected soldier, had served with many men.

"I didn't know that Cowboy fought in the war. World War I — if my math is correct."

"Your math is good, but your logic is not. Think, Kay, think."

I wrestled with remembering the stories Bessie had told me. The words "*But, Rosebud Bend is sacred to those of us whose families fought in the Civil War on the side of the Confederacy. Yes, we lost the battle, but we didn't lose the war … until 1916*" echoed in my mind. Cowboy's war was the Civil War! And, the men with whom he served were still alive today. The toys and trinkets paid homage to the secrets of the sentinels. Yes, each revelation from Bessie had a purpose. I had to sharpen my wits.

The hot sun beat down upon my head. As usual, Bessie had dressed perfectly for the occasion and looked as cool as a cucumber, but I melted. Time to return to the Jeep.

The clock read 3:00 pm. Viva might be home by now, but I would take that chance. I wanted Bessie to read more of her letters in the box.

"Ready to head home?" I asked.

"Not really, dear. I am ready for a sandwich and a cool drink," she replied with a smile.

Time had flown by. I had forgotten all about lunch.

"Where to?" I asked.

"Let's just get some fixings and go to your house. I'm not too old to make a sandwich and brew tea. Besides, I have more I wish to share ... without Viva around," she added with an air of secrecy. "She's been so touchy lately."

Bessie's sudden shift of loyalty troubled me. Had recent events triggered our new alliance? Perhaps, she had never been truly devoted to her old friend.

I made a quick dash to the Piggly Wiggly, and then we headed straight to the house. I would not miss this chance to hear Viva's letters, and, besides, central air-conditioning would feel like heaven compared to the swamp cooler. Bessie made a platter of triangular sandwiches with every crust trimmed. I brewed the tea. When we finished eating, Bessie found a comfortable chair in the living room while I cleared the table. I hastened to put away the food and wash the dishes, eager to continue reading.

I returned to the living room to find Bessie napping. She looked tiny and frail cocooned in the oversized recliner. Her precious box of letters sitting at the foot of the chair tempted me. I slipped to the floor next to her recliner and slid the box closer. I felt a pang of guilt as I opened it, but she planned to share anyway.

She had turned the letters we had read sideways, so I knew exactly where to begin.

Dear Bessie,

Ora came by today to visit awhile. It seems they had a little excitement in town today. They brought in Ol' Jimmy Don Allen for abusing a five-year-old girl, if you know what I mean. I think he was staying with her family, helping with the farm work. Anyway, they were all out in the fields, leaving the little girl to play by herself. Then Jimmy Don disappeared. Everybody thought he just had gone into the woods to do his business. The little girl's older brother went to check on her and caught him red-handed. He jumped him, pinned him down. The little girl took off running and screaming for her ma and pa. By the time her pa got to the house, Jimmy Don had already broke and run. Took to the woods for real this time.

Cowboy rounded up a posse, and they took out after him. Caught Jimmy in the holler just below the house. They hogtied him and took him in. He sat in jail, waiting for the judge to come by. Well, he escaped late that night and ran behind the jail trying to get away. Cowboy just happened to be sittin' behind the jail. Said he was peeling an apple with his knife when Jimmy Don ran smack dab into his blade. Dark as midnight on a moonless night, he said. Ora told me Cowboy said there was nothin' he could do to save him. Just a terrible accident. Ha! No accident there. Cowboy took care of the problem without having to bother the judge. I can tell you straight, there has been little trouble since Cowboy's been the sheriff.

That's all for now. Have to get up early tomorrow, so I need to turn in.

Write soon,
Viva

Lord, have mercy! Who was this man? Did he want justice for a child, or did he murder in cold blood? Two men had lost their lives in that jail, both deaths intertwined with Cowboy, and no one cried foul.

I grabbed the next letter. I could not read fast enough to satisfy my curiosity.

Dear Bessie,

All is well with me and mine. Just a few dust-ups with Darrell. Sometimes I wonder if I am too old to raise a teenage boy. He sneaks off at night and goes over to meet up with Granny Snow's boy, Buddy. I think they roam the woods, treeing coons, or something. He might stay gone till the break of day. And me, with no sleep, worrying about him. I'd take a switch to him, but he's bigger than me. Guess it's just the way with boys. But, it's about to wear this old woman out.

I'm still working at the motel. Got a raise last week. It's still hard to make ends meet with a growin' boy eating me out of house and home, but I wouldn't give him back on a bet. Sometimes Ora hints Cowboy would like him back since all but one of his boys are grown and gone. I think the youngest is still at home. He's the same age as Darrell. Ora's not so keen on it, though. Says she raised all the boys she ever wanted to.

I think it would be a lot easier raising boys with a man in the house. Not something I know as a fact, just guessing.

Enough for now. Write when you can.

Viva

Viva had told me that Joseph did not want Ora to have Darrell. I had always faulted Cowboy, but this letter made me doubt my assumption. Perhaps Joseph thought, "*Ora Price was the cause of it all,*" just like Ezra had. The nuances of the letters were more telling than all of Viva's conversations.

I slid the next letter out of the box.

Dear Bessie,

I am so sorry about the loss of your son. War is a terrible animal that feeds on our young like hounds out of hell. You've lost both of your men to war. It's a shame one person has to sacrifice so much. I know how proud you were of him. He made me proud, too. I really have no words except I know how you're feeling. I know the pain of losing someone you love so dearly. God be with you, dear friend. I wish I could be there with you.

Love as always,
Viva

"Yes, I lost my son in the … what did they call it … the Second World War?"

Bessie's words shattered the spell. I had not heard her stir. Captivated by these age-old letters, I hadn't realized I read this one aloud until she spoke. She showed no sign of anger or betrayal at the sight of me reading her precious memories without permission. I felt more guilt from her lack of reproach than if she had sliced me into tiny pieces with her tongue.

I glanced over my shoulder to see her bottom lip quivering, and her eyes puddled with tears.

"I am so sorry, Bessie," I said as I shifted my gaze. The puddles had turned to streams down her cheeks. I would let the woman grieve in peace.

A long silence lingered between us.

"He didn't die the way everyone thinks he did," she said flatly.

I couldn't imagine what she meant, but with all the secrets surrounding these people, her declaration didn't shock me.

"Please tell me, Bessie. I want to hear about it."

She sat at the edge of the recliner, resting her forearms on her stick-thin legs. "My boy came back from World War II alive and well, in his body that is. But, his insides changed. He had a meanness about him that scared me to the bone. Of course, I still loved him. A mother always loves her son."

Forlorn words of a mother trying to reassure her own doubts.

"He had a wife and a young son. Before the war, they

were so happy. When he returned, he took to drinking." She shook her head as if she struggled to say what came next. "They would get into awful fights and, sometimes, he would hit her. The last time he hit her, she took the baby and went home to her folks. Her dad warned my son if he ever hit her again, he would kill him." She wiped a tear from her cheek. "He didn't wait until the next time. That night, her dad and two brothers snuck up behind the house. My boy was sitting on the back porch, passed out from liquor. They shot him in the back of the head. Her dad claimed it was self-defense and got probation for manslaughter."

Bessie's vivacious spirit had given way to the soft, form-less vulnerability of a painful truth.

"The war claimed my baby just the same as if someone shot him dead in battle." She clenched her teeth behind her closed lips. "When a man kills another man, whatever the reason, a poison gets inside his head and eats away at his soul. Death begets death, in one way or another. My boy's father-in-law was soaked in this poison. It's what caused him to kill my son."

I nodded in silent acknowledgment, at a loss for words.

"Viva said you lost two men to war. Did you have other children?"

"No, I lost my husband during the occupation after World War I. The war to end all wars only ended his life. I've lost all my men to battle."

"What about your grandson?"

"My son's wife turned bitter and scared. I know she loved him. I don't think it crossed her mind that her dad would kill him. Anyway, the family wouldn't let me see the boy. I sent him cards on his birthday and a gift each year for Christmas.

I'm not sure if he ever got them. Never heard a word. They lived in Marlin, so my friends let me know how he was doing." She swallowed hard. "Then, on March 17, 1960, I picked up a newspaper with a headline that read, 'Woman and Child Killed in Head-On Collision.' That child was my grandson."

My heart ached for Bessie. This woman had lost so much: a husband, a son, and a grandson. They say life is not fair, but this woman had experienced three lifetimes full of tragedy. How could one go on after all that?

"Bessie, I don't know how you bear it all. Do you ever just want to give up?"

She flashed me a weak smile. "Every day, dear. Every day. But, each morning I make a choice. I can give in to the grief, or I can keep fighting. I choose to fight. What I've been through can help someone. That's all I have left."

"So, Viva is on a quest to find the truth about Cowboy, and you plan to help her?"

"That's not what I said." She cupped my shoulder, and I felt her bird-like bones under the surface of her skin. "Darrell has tasted the poison of death, too. It runs deep in him." Her eyes bore in as if they saw right into my soul. "I'm not here to help Viva. I'm here to help *you*."

Her words stunned me. The circumstances of Ezra's death and the accusations made about Ora were a burden to Darrell, but why would he have tasted the poison of death, and why did I need help?

"I don't understand. Why would you say that?" I tried to hide my distress.

"All in good time, dear. This tempest has been brewing for over a hundred years. You will not solve it in a day."

Once again, Bessie reminded me I would not push these

ladies. She stood and gathered her letters and box. I knew we needed to return to Viva's, and I dreaded the reunion. Would it be rigid with tension, or would Viva erase the events that displeased her, going on as if nothing had happened? I suspected it would be the latter.

# Chapter XIV

By the time we arrived at the farm, pitch-black darkness swallowed the valley. Lights from the kitchen provided the only evidence that a trail led to a house.

"Sit still, Bessie. I'll come around, and we can walk together."

She could easily trip on the overgrown path scattered with rocks. I stepped into the inky darkness, devoid of chirping katydids and croaking frogs. A piercing scream sliced the silence, followed by a guttural human groan.

"Viva!" I took off running, electrified by fear.

I burst into the kitchen to find Viva staring out the screen door of the back porch. She snapped around, startled. Her jaw dropped, gaping like a fish. She quickly removed her apron and threw it across a pile of dirty dishes by the sink. Clearly, I had interrupted something.

"Are you all right?" I said, breathlessly.

She lifted her nose in the air as if I had just insulted her. "Of course. Why wouldn't I be all right?" The testiness in her voice stopped me cold.

"I thought I heard something ... someone crying out. I don't know. I just wanted to make sure you were okay."

"Where's Bessie?" She turned her back to me as she busied herself at the sink.

Good heavens! I had left her sitting alone in the Jeep. I dashed through the dining room when I spied her dainty frame in the doorway.

"I'm right here, ladies." Bessie wiped her feet on the welcome mat. "None the worse for the wear, unless you count these sandburs on my pant leg." Her lighthearted words belied the somber expression on her face.

"You girls get yourself a plate," Viva called from the kitchen. "I got hungry and ate without you, but there's plenty left."

My eyes followed Bessie's to a large platter dwarfing two pieces of fried chicken and a half-empty bowl of corn on the cob in the middle of the table. I glanced back at the kitchen. Three clean plates stood in the drainboard by the sink. Viva had laid out a feast fit for the prodigal, but he had come and gone.

I thought I would burst with the questions in my mind. *I know I heard a struggle. Who was in trouble? Why was I like Kendra? What poison of death haunted Darrell? How would Cowboy bring solace to my troubled husband? Could Ora have caused it all?* I reminded myself of Bessie's words. *"All in good time, dear."* I had no choice but to accept the admonishment for now. The elephant in the room sat quietly in the corner, as we ate our meager fare.

Exhaustion plagued the lot of us. After clearing the table, we scattered to our respective rooms. Again, sleep eluded me, but the dark solitude quieted my troubled mind until the streaks of light appeared again in the distance. They resembled the beacon of a lighthouse, calling the lost to safety. I turned away from the window. My imagination did not need stirring at this hour.

The morning brought a repeat of yesterday. I rose early only to meet Bessie at the bottom of the stairs. Today, her wide-brimmed hat had natural hues that coupled nicely with a pale blue, fitted linen shirt. Jeans, sneakers, and sunglasses completed her outfit. The finished product had a casual air that hinted we had a new destination.

I accepted Bessie as my sidekick. She had no horse in this race. The rest of us carried a predisposition about the outcome. She did not appear to have any ties except the love for a dear friend.

"Where to today?" I asked.

"Let's go to Pollyanna first." She pushed her shoulders back. "Then we'll figure it out."

I knew Bessie had already decided, but all in her time.

I felt like a regular at the quaint little café. We strolled to the back booth again, and Bessie ordered the same toast and coffee. I had no appetite. Coffee would do this morning. I paid little attention to the surroundings until Bessie nudged me.

"Look," she said.

A similar group of men occupied the corner booth. The same neatly groomed gentleman controlled the hushed conversation. I whipped my head back around to avoid being chastised by my friend.

"The Jeep," I said. "We will talk there."

I finished my much-needed coffee, and we left.

"Okay, Bessie. What *is* this all about?"

"I told you yesterday. That man is a friend of Darrell's."

I smacked my forehead with my palm. "Yes, but so what?"

"Do you know him?"

"No, but I don't know all of Darrell's friends, and he doesn't know all of mine."

Another little white lie had passed my lips. I had no friends in Barber. I only had Darrell's family.

"Is he a work friend?" I asked, hoping.

"No, dear," she murmured. "It's deeper than that. I have seen him come around Viva's at night, knocking on the back door. Darrell goes out, then comes back after a while. He is not a sentinel. Maybe he's a treasure hunter. Doesn't look right to me."

I had to agree. I had never seen that man at my house.

"What are *you* thinking?" I asked.

Bessie's lips curled into a frown. "I don't know what to think, but after last night I know it's not right."

We left it at that. It could be harmless. *Stop*, I told myself. *Of course, it is harmless, but could he have been at Viva's last night? If so, who was with him? I counted three plates. I would ask Darrell about this man when he got home.*

"I want to go to Race Horse Creek before the sun gets any higher," Bessie announced.

So, she knew about Race Horse Creek. There were no surprises when it came to my friend. Race Horse Creek it would be.

I had memorized the road to the creek, as I had passed it several times on my way to Granny's. I started to pull over as we approached.

"Wait!" Bessie cried. "Keep going."

I jerked the wheel back on the road. Irritation burned under my skin. I wished she would stop these outbursts in the middle of my driving, but I kept moving as instructed.

We soon passed the holler by Granny's house. The road made a sharp turn to the left, and we wound up at a steep incline.

"This is Sugar Loaf Mountain," Bessie spoke as if I should know what that meant. "Cowboy and Ora lived on the other side, near to Granny Snow's place. But, it sure was hard to get to.

"Cowboy hated cars. Wouldn't ride in one. He'd take that wagon of his to town, shotgun across his knees, and a load of kids in the back. Hitched his horse in front of the general store. If anyone parked there, the owner of the store booted them out. No one took Cowboy's place."

Cowboy almost sounded like royalty. I tried to picture Cowboy in his buckboard, hauling a passel of kids in the back with a shotgun across his lap. That would be difficult.

We crested the mountain and descended on the other side. The drive was rugged but beautiful. The dogwoods were past their bloom, but the honeysuckle thrived in the heat, perfuming the air with a subtle, sweet fragrance. Tall pines hugged the road as if jealous of the intrusion. At the next turn, the forested path gave way to an expansive lake. Towering cliffs and boulders butted up against the waterline, leaving reflections on the glassy surface of the water.

"Fire and brimstone filled these hills during the Civil War." Bessie swept her hand across the expansive view of the Ozarks. "Arkansas seceded from the Union in 1861, but not all of Arkansas wanted to join the Confederacy. Both sides craved control of Arkansas because of the Mississippi River. Twenty-six thousand men fought the Battle of Pea Ridge in March of '62." She sighed. "The Confederacy lost."

Bessie seemed to love the Confederacy and losing those men must have evoked a sorrow reminiscent of the loss of her son and husband.

"The Union pushed on south and west in December of '62," Bessie continued, "and took Fort Smith in the battle of Prairie Grove. But, they didn't get all the state. Our men dug into these mountains like a tick on a hound dog." Her eyes shimmered with glee. "They sucked the Union blood like a tick, too. Our boys raided at night and hid the loot in caves and mines all over these hills. Remember, Kay, the Union won the battle but didn't win the war. They ruined our chance to take Missouri, but the James boys made up for that."

Bessie delivered her lecture on Civil War history with all the pride of a true Confederate woman. The battle had ended, but the war still raged in her heart. I remembered the letter about how dangerous the hill people became after the war ended, and I remembered Bessie telling me how, despite a victory, the Union did not win the war. Slowly, but surely, Bessie had woven Cowboy's lineage into a tapestry of defiance and survival.

"Cowboy's place is about twenty feet under over there," she said, pointing to the water's edge.

"Underwater?"

She bobbed her head. "Yes. There is more to the story there, too. But, it is time to drive over to Race Horse Creek. It's not getting any cooler."

I backtracked at a leisurely pace, studying the rough terrain. Darrell told me a lot of mines existed here, most abandoned now. Natural caves tucked in the crevices of large boulders, sometimes hidden by the curtain of a waterfall. I could see it all. Beauty and danger occupied the same house.

Race Horse Creek coursed through the rocky foothills of Sugar Loaf Mountain. The roiling water gurgled an invitation. Bessie climbed out and searched for a walking stick. She latched onto a crooked stick stout enough for her purpose, and off we went. She led the way down the rough incline; the same incline I visited my first time here. The path led to the flat sandstone rock with the strange carvings.

"Bessie, this rock looks like the one I found at Rosebud Bend. Does it mark a sentinel's treasure?"

She burst out laughing so hard it took several seconds for her to answer.

"Dear, these are the carvings of children. Guess they heard folks talking." Another giggle escaped her lips. "No self-respecting sentinel would leave a marker out in plain sight."

Just about the time I started to like Bessie, she would get under my skin like a chigger. *Oh, jeez,* I thought, *I'm thinking and talking like her.* Chigger had never been in my vocabulary before.

"I found it in plain sight at Rosebud Bend," I said defensively.

"The river washed the soil away. Now, let's go."

I had my marching orders. I followed Bessie along the river bank. As we rounded a turn in the creek bed, she balanced on a large rock.

"Look up there." She pointed to a crooked tree with the walking stick. "That's a mark of a sentinel. They would bend a sapling to point in the right direction."

"Right direction for what?"

"The next clue," she grumbled in exasperation.

She continued in the direction appointed by the sapling, then stopped and poked around in some loose rocks on a ledge. Her poking produced nothing of value.

"It's no use. I am too old to remember all the signs. We need a map."

I thought about the map in Granny's purse. Could it be

the treasure map of a sentinel? I didn't want to disclose its existence to anyone, and I could not bear to appear naïve a second time.

We trudged back to the Jeep. I made a mental note to purchase a wide-brimmed straw hat and a pair of sunglasses tomorrow.

"Are you ready to call it a day? I have wilted," I said as we climbed back in the Jeep.

"You're used to air conditioning, aren't you, dear?"

*Chigger, chigger,* I thought as her words pricked me.

"Why, in my old house, all I have is a fan. This heat doesn't bother me," said Bessie, slapping her palm to her chest and shaking her head as if the thought of me being uncomfortable perplexed her. "Let's go to your place again. We still have the makings for a sandwich, and we have lots of letters to read."

We made quick work of lunch so we could dive into more of Viva's letters. As we entered the living room, the afternoon sun filtered through the sheers. I pulled the window shade halfway, and we both settled into the recliners on either side of the fireplace.

"Do you remember where we left off, Kay?"

How could I forget? Bessie's boy had died. My irritation with her dwindled as I remembered the pain etched across her face.

Bessie pulled a letter from the box and handed it to me. "You read this time, dear."

Dear Bessie,

Hope this letter finds you well. Glad to hear you're keeping yourself busy. I'd like to tell you time heals all wounds, but it doesn't. Idle time just lets the memory and the loneliness grow like a nasty weed spreading across your lawn. Best to keep your mind busy, so you don't have time to think about your son. That's what I did when Bud died. I still miss him every day.

Sure could use him right now. Heavens to Betsy, I wish you were closer. Be thankful you raised a boy when you were younger. I worry about Darrell. He still goes off nights and might not come home for two or three days at a time. No note, not a word, nothing. What is he up to? It can't be any good. At first, I thought he might be sneaking off to see Cowboy – but now I don't think so. He's still runnin' with Buddy, Granny's son. My boy will be the death of me.

Seems like all I do is complain in my letters, but not much right is happening. I'll close for now. Write soon.

Praying for you,
Viva

Viva's closings had turned affectionate after the passing of Bessie's son. She could be blunt, almost harsh, but she truly loved her friend. Darrell had become more rebellious, but that seemed natural at thirteen. These peeks into his past interested me but did not cause alarm. He was just a normal boy.

I read several more letters from Viva. Most of them lamented the trials of raising a spirited child. I awaited the next Cowboy story. Luckily, it sat atop the pile.

Dear Bessie,

Ora came by today. She looks a little frazzled. Seems they had another tussle on the farm. Cowboy and his boys were out working the field. They broke some new ground and had a lot of rock clearing to do. It won't matter how many acres he breaks if it don't rain. Won't be any crops no how. Well, anyway, it seems Cowboy caught sight of two men skulking about the hay barn down in the meadow. He sent the boys skedaddling to the house. Told them to take care of their ma and the girls and not to leave the house till he got back. Ora said he didn't come home until after dark with his shirt torn and his hand bloodied. All he would say is they won't be bothering anybody anymore.

Can you imagine? I asked if she felt afraid while Cowboy was gone. She said no, she just took out her Bible and prayed.

That's Ora for you. My goodness, for such a godly woman, she can sure swing a switch like the devil if her boys get out of line. Ha!

As usual, not much happening here. If I didn't have Ora and Darrell, I would have very little news to speak of.

Write when you can.

Viva

*Death shadowed Cowboy, but Ora seemed impervious to the depth of the danger*, I thought as I waited with eagerness for Bessie to produce the next piece of the story.

Bessie's rummaging halted. She fidgeted with a letter, reluctant to hand it over.

"Let's call it a night, dear. It's late, and I am tired."

She couldn't fool me.

"Give me the letter," I said, extending my arm.

"Not now, dear."

"Give me the letter."

The sharpness of my voice surprised me. It might have surprised Bessie, too. She clutched the letter against her chest. I felt like a bully hounding a kid for his lunch money.

"Let me have the letter now," I demanded.

She closed her eyes and exhaled before forking over the yellowed page.

Dear Bessie,

Got news of Joseph today. The word's not good. Ora got a letter from an insane asylum somewhere in Illinois. It said Joseph died. Mercy, mercy, he was younger than me! Ora said he plum lost his mind after the fire. She said it was merciful that the Lord had taken him and put him out of his misery. Now, I ask you, don't you find that a strange thing for a mother to say about her son? You should know. You lost your son not too long ago. Ora says the Hackers are cursed with craziness. She thought Ezra was crazy too, taking his own life like that. Yet, last month, she was telling me she was the reason Ezra died. Maybe she's crazy, too. Anyway, I don't want Darrell to hear any of this. He's hard enough to handle as it is without the excuse of being crazy himself.

Well, it's time for me to turn in. Morning still comes early. Write when you can.
Bye for now.


                                            Viva


The letter shook in my grasp at the implication. I lifted my gaze, almost afraid to speak the thoughts that danced in my mind. "Bessie, does Viva think Darrell's crazy?"

"Aren't we all a little crazy, dear?" She shrugged. "Don't let your imagination run away with you." She waved me off with a flick of her wrist. "I shouldn't have shown you that letter. We've got more to worry about than that right now."

I remained unconvinced by her flimsy reasoning, but maybe she was right. If we could call anyone crazy, it would be me. I had given up a perfectly good career to marry a man I hardly knew. Now, I spent my days talking with old women about rocks and a man named Cowboy. Nevertheless, I could not let the mystery of Ezra go. Talk about crazy. I still felt tiny tugs of doubt about Darrell. His actions and reactions to Cowboy were odd, to say the least.

As if to entice me out of dark speculations, Bessie held another letter in front of me.

"Here, dear. Read the next one."

Dear Bessie,

Well, I went to a rodeo dance tonight. Can you imagine that? My legs are stove-up, and I can't dance a lick – but I went anyway. Darrell's taken a fancy to some young lady named Kendra. He wanted to meet up with her at the dance. I wasn't about to let him go alone. I told him the only way he could go was if I went too. He pouted, but he knew I meant it. Guess I didn't know what I had been missing. Mercy, they had piles of food and straw bales lined up along the walls. They had it in an old barn at the rodeo grounds. I sat and ate and watched all the dancing. They had a little moonshine going on out back, too. Some of those fools sure could dance with a little liquor in 'em. Ha!

The best surprise of all was Cowboy. Ora never told me he played a fiddle. He sure could make that catgut sing. He played polkas and waltzes and country swing music way into the night. He wore me plum out, but I had so much fun. That is until I couldn't find Darrell. I guess he snuck out right under my nose. Thought he took off with Kendra, but I saw her with her folks in the far corner.

I didn't see hide nor hair of that boy until the next morning. He found me waiting up for him on the couch when he came in. When he saw me, his face got rock hard and red as a beet. He clenched his teeth and hissed, "Get out of the way, old woman." The hair on the back of my neck stood straight up. He scares me, Bessie. He's nineteen and big and strong like his daddy. I don't know how long I can stand this. What am I doing wrong, Bessie? What am I doing wrong?

    Sorry to bother you with my problems, but I need your help.

Write when you can.


                          Viva


Wow! These vicious words from my mild-mannered husband made the hair on the back of *my* neck stand up. I could only imagine how Viva must have felt. Where were the traces of belligerence now? I had never seen this side of Darrell.

"What did you tell her?" I asked. That letter begged a response.

"I told her to stay out of his way. Let him go." She pursed her lips. "Those were not the ways of a rebellious teen. Darrell's hatred oozed out of him like pus from a wound."

 "Did she let him go?"

What a stupid question. I knew how close Darrell and Viva were now. W*eren't they*?

"She did what most mothers do," said Bessie. "She ignored me completely and kept trying to help the boy."

"Did it work?"

I had just asked another stupid question.

Bessie shifted in her chair. We had been sitting for a long time, and this conversation had taken a turn in a dark direction faster than people raced out of church on a sultry Sunday in August.

"For a while. A few months later, they had another blowup. This time he beat her. Bruises all over and a broken tooth. Cut her lip pretty bad, too."

The bile rose in my throat, and it burned as I swallowed it down. My feelings for Darrell took a seismic shift for the worse. I kneeled on the floor in front of Bessie.

"I'll ask you again," I said, despite being terrified of the answer. "Is Darrell crazy?"

Bessie's gaze never left my face. "Crazy has no intent, my dear. Darrell is a deliberate man."

I shuddered at the chill racing through my bones.

"If what you are saying is true, then I can't stay with Viva or Darrell any longer."

My words sounded overdramatic, but Darrell's past reinforced how little I knew about my husband. He and I needed to talk. My desire for a warm, loving family had clouded my judgment. I had given up a quiet, boring life for an illusion that harbored evil and violence.

"You'll stay right where you are, dear."

"I won't," I whimpered.

"You will!" The whispery southern drawl had vanished as Bessie drilled her finger into the arm of the chair.

"But, how?" I cried. "How can I pretend that this Darrell doesn't exist? How can I look at Viva and not see the pain he put her through?"

"Don't make more of it than what it is."

Bessie's answer gave me whiplash. She did a one-eighty is less than five minutes.

"Kay, I didn't mean to scare you, but you need to know these things for your own good. I love you like a daughter. Trust me."

A coquettish grin crossed her lips, easing my distrust. This sweet southern wisp of a woman would never cause me harm, but the undercurrents surrounding Darrell disturbed me. *Fly under the radar*, I reminded myself. *Stay under the radar*

# Chapter XV

The next morning brought relief. Bessie did not lurk at the bottom of the stairs, and I didn't see Viva anywhere. Today, I would visit Granny again. I had no invite, but I would deal with that when the time came.

With the morning fresh and bright, I found Granny resting on the east porch in the shade of the whitewashed shotgun house. A Bluetick hound lounged at her feet, oblivious to my approach.

"Good to see you, missy. I gave up on you," she said.

I tilted my head to one side. "Why would you give up on me?"

"Buddy kept calling the *Gazette*, but no one ever answered."

Oh, my. I had completely forgotten about the *Gazette*. The paper only had three employees. The owner took charge of integrating AP stories that made headlines each week. Carolyn created the local ads and booked subscriptions. That left me to cover local reporting and community columns.

We lacked a formal structure, but I never missed a deadline. This was Wednesday, and the layout had to be done tonight to make the weekly paper. I would deal with that later. Right now, I needed to speak with Granny.

"Come sit." She patted the rocker next to hers. "Let's talk."

The temperature had cooled this morning. It would be a good day to slip off your shoes and enjoy life. But, I had a mission.

"Now, where did we leave off?" she asked.

That Granny had no recollection of where our last conversation began or ended gave me a chance to guide her. I never claimed to be a scholar, but I knew my history pretty well. I needed to know more about the infamous Jesse James and Cowboy.

"I know Jesse James was an outlaw from Missouri," I started, "and I think he was Jesse Cole's father."

"You *know* … you *think* … you don't *know* nothing, missy. What I am about to tell you isn't found in history books. Those books never had much use for the truth."

Her words piqued my curiosity.

"The Jesse you know is Jesse R. James, not Jesse Woodson James. Why, Jesse R. was just a little bandit from Missouri." She lifted her hand, palm facing me as if stopping traffic. "Just a minute, missy."

"Buddy," Granny yelled. "Buddy!"

A moment later, the large man who resembled Skeeter appeared at the screen door. He said nothing.

"Go get Granny that piece of paper in her top dresser drawer. You know, the one folded like this."

Granny motioned for me to give her a piece of notebook paper. She then folded it neatly into quarters.

"And, Buddy, there's a big *J* and a big *R* on the back."

At her odd instructions, Buddy nodded and left, returning in a few minutes with the document.

She handed me a copy of the 1850 census in Clay County, Missouri. The paper was weathered and brittle with age. Halfway down the page, my eyes landed on the name Jesse R. James, age 4. No other name had a middle initial, and no Jesse Woodson James appeared on the census.

I remembered Viva's words: *"Well, she didn't know much about him, but Cowboy told her one thing before the marriage. She said he looked her straight in the eye and told her that his father was Jesse Woodson James and that there would always be grave danger if she married him. He called attention to the middle name like he wanted there to be no confusion with any other man named Jesse James."*

Excited by my discovery, I dropped my pen and watched it roll across the porch. That lifeless hound jumped into action, snatching the pen in his teeth. Granny's laughter spooked the dog, and he took off, running into the woods. I did not care.

Granny stopped laughing and fixed her gaze squarely on my face. "Do you hear what I am telling you, missy?"

I *heard* and *understood*.

"Yes!" My smile stretched ear to ear. "There were two Jesse Jameses."

Granny smacked the arm of her rocker. *I got it!*

"There were a lot more than two. I got this from Pa years ago," she said, waving the census up and down. "Pa said not to let this out to anyone. It would only cause trouble. Some people figured the 'R' came from his brother Robert, who I heard was born in July of 1845. Census takers do make errors, but that's a stretch. No, these people are not Jesse Woodson James's direct kin. These people are that little bandit Jesse R's folks."

Could the census be that flawed? Or could Cowboy's Jesse James have been the head of the KGC? I doubt that Viva had the answer. Granny took me deep into the web surrounding the James family, and the revelations boggled my mind.

"This Jesse Woodson James also had a brother named Frank, who was my pa, and he took the name of Joe Vaughn. They came from Kentucky just like Jesse R's folks did. The whole passel were cousins who fought alongside Quantrill."

Granny leaned forward and clasped my hand. "I need to know if you believe me. If you don't, we will leave it here."

Oddly enough, I believed her. Cousins with the same names are not uncommon, even today, and the census clearly raised questions about Missouri Jesse. And, now, I had learned that her pa, Joe, was not the Frank that rode with Jesse "R," but the brother of Jesse Woodson James. Granny's claims made sense, and history could only make sense if there were two Jesse Jameses.

"Go on," I said.

"After the war, both Jesses were hell-bent on revenge. Kentucky Jesse and my pa ran the underground while Missouri Jesse robbed banks and trains."

"The underground?"

"The KGC – Knights of the Golden Circle," she said with a huff.

I guess I should have known.

"Pa wrote about all of this in his journal. You see, Jesse R. robbed for the Confederacy, and Jesse Woodson stood guard over the treasure."

*Fascinating. People must know about this. Why had I never heard this story before?*

"That was a long time ago. Did they find all those stockpiles?"

"Some. They buried things all over; New Mexico, Texas, Oklahoma, and some right here in Arkansas."

My thoughts turned to Cowboy. Had he come to Barber to protect the caches of the KGC? Was this why he and Frank James, aka Joe Vaughn, made their way to these Ozark hills? Did this explain the secret meetings between Cowboy and Joe that Granny spoke about? The answer lay buried as deep as their plunder.

"Are there treasures buried near here?" I asked, eager for her reply. This could be the connection I needed to explain why Cowboy would leave the Texas Brazos and make his home in the Arkansas hills.

Granny's eyes drifted across the piney hills and valleys. She appeared transfixed, lost in reflection. I felt her weigh the cost of telling the truth, whatever it may be. The story belonged to Granny, to share or not to share. I dared not speak for fear I would break the spell.

Granny spoke slow and deliberate in her nasal backwoods drawl.

"In 1876, a detail of Mexican guards drove a pack train of burros loaded with bullion across the desert. The Missouri James gang attacked. They stole the burros and the bullion, then hightailed it across Texas, headed for Indian Territory. No laws or lawmen in Indian Territory, so if they made it they would be safe. Late in February, our men finally reached the Wichita Mountains."

I noted how she referred to them as "our" men.

"A fierce winter blizzard raged across the mountains." She shuddered as if a cold wind blew up behind us. "They traveled for three and a half days through snow almost a foot deep, hardly stopping to rest. But, Jesse knew their animals couldn't go much farther."

Granny's voice embraced the saga like gentle fingers caressing silk. She spoke each word with the reverence befitting the fine gift of her pa's story. I listened with an intensity worthy of a believer.

"They finally reached a spot east of Cache Creek in the Territory. The men buried some stolen loot in a deep ravine and marked it with two signs pointing to the gold. Jesse nailed a burro shoe on the bark of a cottonwood tree, then he emptied his six-shooter into another cottonwood tree for his second mark. He knew the signs wouldn't last long, but it would do until they came back in the spring.

Before they rode out of the storm, Jesse etched an outlaws' contract on the side of a brass bucket with an old hammer and tack. The contract bound each member of the gang to secrecy. Frank and Jesse buried the bucket somewhere on Tarbone Mountain."

It intrigued me to know outlaws wrote a contract legally binding other outlaws. I guess honor among thieves existed.

"What did the contract say?"

"Buddy," Granny Snow called out. "Buddy."

He lumbered into the doorway with Granny's summons.

"Go get me pa's journal. You'll find it in that same drawer, only it's a little black book about this size," she said, outlining the dimensions in the air with her fingers.

Buddy left without saying a word.

Granny spoke slow and plain to Buddy, almost as if to a child. I realized I had never heard Buddy speak, except to say, *"Come in"* or *"Go home."*

After Buddy returned with the journal, Granny flipped through the book until she arrived at a dog-eared page of faded writing.

"Here it is," she said as she began to read the contract aloud.

> "This, the 5th day of March 1876, in the year of our Lord, 1876, we the undersigned do this day organize a bounty bank. We will go to the west side of the Keechi Hills, which is about fifty yards from (symbol of crossed sabers). Follow the trail line coming through the mountains just east of the lone hill where we buried the jack (burro). His grave is east of a rock. This contract made and entered into this V day of March 1876. This gold shall belong to who signs below."

A list of names scratched into the bucket followed: Jesse James, Frank Miller, George Overton, Rub Busse, Charlie Jones, Cole Younger, Will Overton, Uncle George Payne, Frank James, Roy Baxter, Bud Dalton, and Zack Smith.

The archaic language filled my ears with foreign phrases. This band of outlaws wove references to the Lord, bounty banks, crossed sabers, and jack burros, with the Roman Numeral V to memorialize the contract of thieves. I had not imagined these men as religious and educated.

"What happened next, Granny? You said they buried *some* gold."

"They only needed to lighten their load and rest their animals. Winter blows in fast and furious on the plains, and it leaves just as quickly. When the storm broke, they took off eastward toward the Ouachita Mountains and held up at

Robber's Cave for several days. They didn't want to risk going back to the Wichita's, so they headed north. They intended to go back to Tarbone Mountain later in the year."

"North, to where Granny?"

"They came here, missy. They came here. They split up the bullion and buried it in small hideaways throughout these hills to throw people off the mark, but they buried most of it in an old mining cave near Sugar Loaf Mountain. Six months later, the James gang got ambushed while robbing the Northfield bank up in Minnesota. Jesse escaped, but he didn't get his share before Bob Ford shot him dead."

I shivered as chills ran up my spine. Granny revealed that two Jesses resisted the Union and concealed their bounty in these hills. The hidden treasure demanded an unspoken pact of silence between Granny and me about the secrets cradled in this valley of the Ozarks.

"I remember from history classes that Bob Ford murdered Jesse James. What a terrible way for Jesse Cole's dad to die!"

I hoped I sounded knowledgeable.

"Not Jesse *Woodson* James, missy. Jesse R. died at the hands of Bob Ford. Come with me. Buddy can't fetch what I need to show you."

We started toward Granny's bedroom through a hall lined with rows of pictures hanging in crude pine frames. Many had the glossy shine of photographs, but someone had cut others out of newspapers or magazines. Why frame old newspaper and magazine pictures?

"This is Jesse James, this is Jesse James, and this is Jesse James," Granny said, pointing at the first, second, and third frames. Down the hall, she ambled, tapping each framed image for emphasis.

I studied the pictures carefully as I walked up and down the hall. Some resembled each other, but most were pictures of totally different people.

"Granny, these are not the same people."

She laughed. "No, they're not, missy. But, all the 'so-called' experts swear they are. And, they call *me* crazy!"

"What are you trying to say? You told me they're Jesse James, and now you are telling me they aren't."

She planted a hand on each hip. "What I am telling you *is* that a lot of men claimed to be Jesse, and the people they robbed swore they were, too. If you are robbed, it might as well be by a famous outlaw. Sure makes a better story to tell. No one wants to be taken by a two-bit drifter," she said with a know-it-all grin.

"Look again and tell me how many men you see."

I leaned in closer so I could study the nuances of each face. "There are at least three or four different people," I replied.

"At least," she agreed, "but someone swore that every one of these men was *the* Jesse James. They might have been members of his gang, but there is only one *Jesse Woodson James*. Cowboy knew. My pa knew. That's all that matters. Come, I want you to see something else."

Granny dug through her top dresser drawer, pushing piles of paper to the side.

"Here it is. Now, look at this. Look at how he describes Jesse." She pointed to the words underlined in pencil.

Granny handed me a copy of the transcript from Frank James' trial.

4© Dick Liddil Testimony -The roads were so muddy that we went back, Jesse and myself, to the old lady; Wood and Frank to the Fords'; and Clarence to Mrs. Samuels. We stayed there for three or four days. Shortly after this, we started again. Four went horseback and one on the cars. Wood went on the train. We came up to this county to look out for a place to take a train. Frank was riding a roan pony. He took her at Richmond, and Wood Hite had a little bay mare, taken at the same time. Jesse and I had the horses we rode on during the previous trip. The horses gotten at Liberty were turned loose at Richmond. We started that night, and camped out before daylight, somewhere in the woods. We were to meet Wood Hite at Gallatin. We stopped and had dinner with a Dutchman in a one-story frame close to the road, with a large barn one hundred yards from it. He had a family of five or six children. He had several fine cows and sold milk at Kidder. I left my leggings there and had to go back after them. I reckon this place was ten or fifteen miles from Gallatin. At that time I had short whiskers all over my face. Jesse was five feet eleven inches and a half high, round face, pug nose, dark sandy whiskers, and blue eyes. He weighed 195 pounds and stood very straight. Frank James had burnsides and mustache. His whiskers were darker than his mustache. From that German's we went to Gallatin, first stopping in the timber to wait for Wood Hite. This was almost a mile from the town, on the road to Winston. I have never been to the place since.

Dick Liddil, a traitorous member of the James gang, had turned on Jesse and Frank. *What might Granny want me to understand from all of this?*

I shrugged. "Okay, what is the point?"

"The man's hair in the casket is black. Dick Liddil said Jesse had dark sandy whiskers and blue eyes — not black, like this picture. Some said he dyed his hair, but no one made a mention of that when they laid him out for burial. They just made the story fit what they wanted to believe. The real Jesse Woodson James lived long after Bob Ford died."

Granny brought up many things I had never thought about before. People had no identification a hundred years ago. Men could say anything with little chance of being contradicted. Outlaws changed names like dirty shirts. Who could really know how many 'Jesse Jameses' existed? He got around a lot for one man.

"Take a look at this, missy."

I grabbed the handwritten letter.

James (O'Neil)          November 30, 1889.

"I met up with Jesse James not long ago. He is quite a character — you said he was killed in 82. His mother swore that the body in the coffin was his, but it was another man they called Tracy or Lynch. He was a cousin of Wild Bill. He is passing under the name of Dalton, but he can't fool me. I know all of the Daltons, and he sure ain't one of them. He told me he promised his gang and his mother that if he lived to a hundred he would confess. To make it strange, Jesse sang at his own funeral. Poor devil, he can't cod me, not even with his long hair and a billy goats wad of hair on his chin. I expect he will start preachin'. He is smart, maybe he can do it."

Jane

"Who is this person called Jane?" I asked.

"Calamity Jane!" Granny tapped her foot against the floor. "You know, she was a frontier woman and an Indian scout. She knew the real Jesse, all right."

Her demeanor said it all. She had produced an eyewitness of sorts. Calamity Jane had met with Jesse James long after the purported killing of the man. This meant the man in the casket could not be Jesse James, at least not Jesse Woodson James. Could it be Jesse R. or one of the many others who claimed to be the outlaw? Granny must have read the questions bouncing around in my head.

"I could go on and on about this," she said, "but I won't."

"Don't stop there," I pleaded. I did not want to quit without knowing the whole story. "Are you saying the real Jesse James was not murdered in St. Joe, Missouri?"

"Maybe someday we'll talk more about it. If I live long enough." She raised both eyebrows. "We really need to talk about Cowboy. That's why you are here, isn't it?"

Yes, I wanted to know all about Cowboy, but I felt the truth lay buried with the mystery of Jesse Woodson James. I asked once again to no avail. Granny would have no more to do with the assassination of the man from St. Joe.

This convoluted mess that swirled in my brain began with Ezra's forlorn poem etched in the stucco of an old jail cell. My trust in those around me disappeared and led me to question the very foundation of history. Three old women tested every ounce of my sanity.

The hour grew late. I needed to go home to Darrell. *Please let him be home.*

"I will be back in a few days," I told Granny. Her face looked drawn as if she, too, needed a rest.

I made a hasty retreat to my Jeep, ready to mend the breach with my husband.

# Chapter XVI

As the Jeep rounded the corner, I spied Darrell's truck in the driveway. I sighed with relief. I ran into the kitchen and straight into Darrell's arms. He might be the first person under seventy I had seen in days. The intrigue and mystery of the past couple of weeks slipped away. Perhaps out of loneliness, I had let my imagination get away from me. And …

Oh, Lordy! I forgot about the *Gazette*. Darrell's first night home, and I had to work. I feared this would upset him, but he just laughed.

"I have some things to take care of myself," he said. "My desk is probably piled high with emergencies."

What could I say? But, how many emergencies could there be in geology? *Stop it*, I told myself. Bessie, Viva, and Granny Snow, sure had me twisted up.

We shared a small meal and, with a swift peck on the cheek, Darrell sent me on my way.

My eyes widened when I saw the disarray of my desk. I

dropped my shoulders. This pile would take hours to plow through. I made a pot of coffee and settled in for the long haul. I finished in record time, but not before the clock struck one. I snapped back into the present. I had not heard from Darrell, so I swung by his office to keep him company. When I arrived, the pitch-black parking lot did not look promising. Darrell must have headed home already.

I pulled into our driveway. No Darrell. This day had worn me out. I trudged inside and crashed on the couch, waiting for his arrival.

Bright lights jolted me from sleep. I blinked a few times to shake the cobwebs from my brain. Darrell stood over me, his mouth curled into a scowl, and clenched fists hung by his sides.

"Why are you sleeping on the couch? I thought you would be in bed by now," he barked.

A quick glance at the mantle clock confirmed the late hour. Why had he come home at 3:23 AM? *I should be the one upset*, I thought, but he turned the tables on me.

"Where have you been?" I shouted.

My grogginess and his sharp query had prodded me to anger.

Darrell raised his hand as if to strike me, but dropped it just as quickly.

"Stay where you are," he grumbled. "I can find the bedroom by myself." He turned and left, slamming the door behind him.

I knew this Darrell from Viva's letters. His rock-hard jaw and glazed eyes scared me more than his words. The source of his anger escaped me, yet I sensed a real fury. Had he always been this way, or did my nosing in the past bring this rage into my house? Had the abuse turned on me? Bessie hinted more than once that she feared for my safety. Now, I did, too.

After a restless night, I rolled over to find the other side of the bed empty. Darrell's suitcase and toiletry bag that sat on the bedroom floor last evening had disappeared. He had left and appeared to have no intention of returning soon.

My head throbbed as I lay in silence, trying to understand the events from last night. The creaking of the back door interrupted my thoughts. *Darrell came back.* I hoped with every ounce of my being he wanted to work things out. The thud of footsteps echoed down the hall toward the bedroom but stopped short. The peculiar squeak of Darrell's office door followed by the sound of a drawer opening piqued my interest. If he came to see me, why would he go to his office first?

I slipped my bathrobe on and headed to confront him. I pushed the door open.

"What are you looking — " I gasped.

The man bent over the file drawer wore a starched tan shirt with a tie. *The man from the Pollyanna.* He stood and ran toward me, swinging a fist at my face. The blow connected with a mighty force knocking me to the ground. He leaped over me and bounded down the hall and out the back door. The punch had caught me squarely on the cheekbone. I felt my eye swelling as blood trickled from my lip. Weak and disorientated from the assault, fear washed over me. I no longer felt safe in my home. Darrell had taken off, and the man left empty-handed. He would return better prepared next time. I must leave Barber. But, where would I go?

My mind raced through options. *Wait, a minute.* There were no 'options,' only an 'option.' I had no reason to stay in Barber. With no friends here, my only choice would be to return to Little Rock. Leaving would be best. Things had not been right with Darrell and me since Cowboy appeared in my life, so I could not turn to him. For all I knew, he sent the man to the house. I had no way of knowing. Even if I wanted to, I could not undo my actions of the last few weeks. I would share my plans with Granny and Bessie, but I did not trust Viva. A mother's loyalty to her son runs deep.

Catching Bessie without Viva in tow would be a trick. My only hope rested in a grocery store run. Bessie had a penchant for jasmine tea, and Viva seldom obliged. I might see her at the Piggly Wiggly. I sat in the parking lot for hours, hoping for a glimpse of Bessie. I almost missed her. She emerged from a local cab with a magnetic sign stuck to the side. As she waved him on, I latched onto her arm.

"Come with me for a minute." I led her to my Jeep and parked on the far side, a good distance from the grocery store entrance.

"I know why you are here," Bessie said before I could speak. "You're leaving Barber. Now, listen to what I am telling you." She drew in a deep breath and paused. "They will not let you leave," she uttered with resignation.

Her words stunned me. How did she know about last night?

"I am here because a man broke into my home and attacked me," I shrieked.

"The hills have eyes. And, all eyes are on you, dear."

My heart climbed into my throat. How could this be happening? "Me? Why are all eyes on me?"

Her ridiculous words alarmed me.

"Every confidence you shared with Viva and Granny Snow, and every confidence they shared with you, sealed your fate."

"What confidences? All we ever talked about was Cowboy and Jesse James and ... " I paused.

"And, what, dear?" She blinked several times. "The treasure? Darrell? Maps? KGC?"

Bessie's words rang true. Viva and Granny Snow had both warned me.

"You're the one who wanted me to talk to Granny. Why did you do that if it put me in danger?" My voice cracked with annoyance.

"You were knee-deep in danger when I met you," she replied.

The air threatened to stifle me. Beads of sweat dotted my hairline.

"How? Why?" I mumbled.

"When Viva wrote to me that Darrell had a new wife, I had my concerns. But, when you brought Viva to Texas to learn about Cowboy, I knew it was too late. Why do you think I came back to Arkansas with you?"

"To spend time with Viva."

She shook her head. "Dear, Viva and I have been friends for a long, long time. I didn't have to come to Arkansas for friendship. Letters were enough." Her voice softened. "I came to help you."

"Me?" I cried. "Why me?"

"I am afraid for you, Kay. I told you. Darrell has the poison of death in his bones."

I rolled my eyes. The poison of death again. Had she gone crazy?

"I know talk of Ezra upset Darrell, but why would that make you afraid for me? Is it because of the way he treated Viva?" In truth, I feared him after last night, but not in a life or death sort of way. Right now, I feared the man in the tan shirt, but what connection did he have to Darrell?

"It's not Ezra. It's not Viva. Kendra's death poisoned Darrell. There, I've said it." Bessie's mouth twisted in consternation as she braced for my reply.

"Just how did Kendra die? Darrell won't talk about it at

all. Not a word."

My pent-up frustration with the whole situation spewed forth like venom as I gripped the steering wheel. I had vowed never to ask. I wanted to respect Kendra's memory, but the maddening silence surrounding her life and death taxed me beyond endurance.

She placed a hand on my leg. "Most folks believe he killed her."

I fell back against the seat and stared out the windshield. People suspected the man I had married of killing his wife, yet no one had shared an inkling with me. I needed to know more but could not bear to ask. A man, who at the very least was an acquaintance of Darrell, had attacked me. I wanted to head to Little Rock and never look back, but Bessie's words danced in my head. "They will not let you leave."

"What am I going to do? Where will I go?" I stammered once I found my strength.

"You'll go to Granny Snow. She's expecting you. Go home and get your things. Take everything. Head east out of town and double back. It is best if everyone thinks you went to Little Rock." She squeezed my hand. "And, Kay, stay put. I will contact you."

Bessie tucked her pocketbook under her arm and reached for the door.

"Wait! You said you were here to help."

"I am, dear. My body is old, but my mind's not feeble. I know all of their secrets. Trust me."

I grabbed her arm as she moved toward the door again.

"Then why aren't you in danger?" I asked.

Bessie's rosy pink cheeks erupted with a gigantic smile. "Because they think my mind *is* feeble." A hearty chuckle shook her petite frame. "To them, I am just an eccentric old lady in fancy clothes who asks silly questions. I'm not a threat, so everyone talks freely around me. But, I listen." She tapped her ear with a finger. "Old ladies make the best spies. Now, get going," she said with a wink.

Clearly, I had lessons to learn about flying under the radar.

I drove to the house to gather my belongings. Darrell had not returned, which disappointed me. I secretly hoped he would sweep in and explain away everything that had happened in the last two days. I tossed my clothes into a suitcase before turning to personal items. Wedding gifts and furniture held no interest for me, but I wanted my life insurance policy that Darrell kept in his office in the back bedroom. I grabbed the handle and turned the knob, but the door would not budge. Someone had locked it. I raced to the kitchen and grabbed a knife out of the drawer. I jimmied the lock until it opened, leaving a circle of gouges. *He would know I broke in*, I thought, as I dug through the file cabinets.

The mess in his office proved to be an obstacle. Junk mail intermingled with important documents made the task daunting. My nerves did little to expedite the search. I tossed aside the papers I deemed irrelevant as I made my way through the piles.

My heart pounded when I came to a tattered newspaper with letters cut out of the pages, just like the ones on the mysterious letter I had received at the *Gazette*. Did Darrell record the phone messages, too? I had no time to think. I found the insurance policy and stumbled across a file labeled 'Kendra.' I needed to know more about this woman. I took them both.

I did just as Bessie instructed. I headed east toward Little

Rock and doubled back around the lake to Granny's house. As I drove up the hill, I saw Granny sitting on the east porch. Buddy appeared out of nowhere, ready to carry my bags. We emptied the Jeep, and Buddy jumped in and drove toward the old wooden barn. He parked my truck inside and placed a dilapidated farm truck and tractor in front of the barn doors to block the entrance. I retreated to the shotgun shack to find Granny, but she had disappeared, and Buddy never returned from the barn. Exhausted, I plopped down in Granny's rocker. I relinquished my claim of existence to the oppressive silence of this old house.

I tried to make myself at home in the tiny, one-window bedroom, coveting Granny's panoramic view. A blood-red sun descended behind the towering peaks of Sugar Loaf Mountain, casting darkness upon the valley. I heard noises coming from the kitchen. Too fidgety to sit alone, I strolled down the hall. The gauge of a pressure cooker hissed and whistled on the stove, spinning in angry circles while the strange woman from the porch sat hunkered over the kitchen table stemming strawberries. She wore a pink and white striped cotton dress and had secured her dark hair in a ponytail. The woman had never been friendly, but at this point, I did not care. I pulled up a chair at the table beside her.

"I'm Kay," I said as I extended my hand. "I have seen you before, but we've never been introduced. Are you Buddy's wife?" I sounded lame.

"No, ma'am. Buddy's got no wife."

The woman offered nothing else, so I prodded her.

"Are you related to Granny?"

"No, ma'am. I just work here ... three days a week. I'm with county welfare," she said as she handed me a pack of ice wrapped in a rag. "Here, this will take care of that bruise," she said, motioning toward my face.

Her words, although not friendly, had no air of hostility. The cool bundle felt great on my swollen cheek.

"I take care of Granny and Buddy," she added.

"Are you with elder care?"

She shook her head. "No, I'm here for Buddy. Ever since his accident, they've both needed help. I mainly cook, clean ... do the laundry. I try to cook enough for them to have leftovers on my days off, but with Buddy, that's hard. That man eats like a horse." She laughed.

Her lingering smile transformed her face, and I wondered if she might be younger than I first thought.

"I bring the groceries — pay the bills when I come. You know, just the normal stuff."

"What kind of accident did Buddy have?" I asked. I had hints Buddy had problems, but didn't realize he needed a caretaker.

She stiffened as if a bird had flown into the house. "Ma'am, I don't talk about the folks I work for. If you want to know somethin', ask Granny."

Her tone discouraged further conversation. She set the table and left, leaving the food warming in the stove.

I heard Granny stir, and after a bit, she shuffled into the kitchen. Her long grey hair, usually knotted in a neat bun, looked disheveled, with strands trailing every which way.

"Where's Buddy?" I asked as I eyed the battered pork chops and mashed potatoes steaming in the belly of a warm oven.

"He won't be here tonight. We can eat. Just make him a plate for later. He always comes in hungry."

We both had appetites, so we ate in silence. My nerves needed a break to prepare for engaging with Granny, so I avoided conversation.

"Shall we go to the parlor, missy? I think it's cooler in there. There's a cross breeze from the front door through that window." Granny pointed her finger in the window's direction. "That's quite a welt," she added as if an afterthought.

A gentle breeze teased the yellowed lace curtains, providing welcome relief from the evening heat. Granny settled in a well-loved rocker covered with a faded blue cloth. I saw a letter "B" carved into the right arm of the wooden chair, while the left arm carried a scratched letter "D."

*How unusual.* The chair, although not fancy, was certainly a prized piece of furniture in its day. Who would deface it?

Granny caught my stare.

"You're wondering about this," she said, tracing the initials with her finger.

I nodded.

"The 'B' is for Buddy." She looked down as she continued to trace the carvings. "The 'D'…" She glanced up. "Is for Darrell."

She knew the effect this would have on me. My heart raced with realization. Viva had written that Buddy and Darrell ran together, but I had no clue he had been a welcomed guest in her home. I assumed two young boys snuck around and met up at night for coon hunting and the like. It seemed there was a lot more to it. Granny did not trust Darrell. Clearly, she feared the man she knew and not the shadow of a stranger.

"I've known Darrell for a very long time," she said, answering my question before I asked it. "And, I knew you would come here sooner or later."

I bolted out of my chair. "Stop! Just stop for a minute!" All these secrets infuriated me. "My husband stays out all night after being gone for two weeks. He comes home in the wee hours of the morning madder than a wet hornet and leaves me at daybreak. Bessie tells me I can't leave Barber because they won't let me, but I don't even know who *they* are. Then she tells me Darrell killed his wife, that she is afraid for me and, and, and then Bessie tells me to hide out at your house. Now, you are telling me you expected me, and you don't even know Bessie. I want answers," I said through clenched teeth. "I want answers NOW!"

Granny's eyes widened. "You–need–to–calm–down, missy," she said, emphasizing every word. "I asked if you were strong enough to handle all of this, and you said YES."

"Well, that's before I knew 'yes' meant my husband might kill me."

My words sounded silly. Darrell would never entertain something so heinous. I had escaped the bounds of sanity, letting the tales of Cowboy, hangings, treasures, and rocks run amuck. I reined in my fears and started again.

"Forgive me, Granny. I'm acting like a child. My imagination has gotten the best of me." I sat back down. "Why did you expect me?" I asked with a calmness I did not feel.

"Yes, missy. Darrell might … kill you. That's why you're here. Bessie and I are afraid he might. But, we aren't certain."

I took little comfort in Granny's uncertainty. The darkness of the room amplified my fears until I could no longer bear it. I reached to turn on a lamp, hoping the light would chase the shadows from my mind.

"No lights, Kay. No one knows you are here except Buddy, Bessie, and me. I don't burn lights at night. Might make people suspicious."

Granny's words scared me more than the dark. The lights stayed off. I resigned myself to the darkness, but I would not give up on finding answers. The mystery of the jailhouse hanging and Cowboy had evolved into a fight for my life. I swallowed my fears, hoping the sane processes of my training would take control.

"How do you know Bessie?" I asked.

"Do you remember pa's night meetings I told you about? I only knew one man that came to see pa. Jesse Woodson James. He had Cowboy with him most of the time. I only caught sight of him once or twice, but it was Cowboy all right. Tall and slender, he stood out from the rest of 'em. Not likely to forget him. Didn't see him for many years, but I recognized him right away when he came to Barber."

"What were those meetings about?" I thought I knew the answer, but I wanted her to say it.

"The treasure, of course."

"That doesn't explain how you knew Bessie."

She waved her hand at me. "Slow down, missy. I'm getting to that. You see, Cowboy headquartered at the Bar Seven Ranch near Waco. He wandered all over northern Texas and Indian Territory doing work for the KGC. Bessie's pa was his partner."

So, Bessie's father carried the banner of a sentinel. I should have guessed her interest in the war and the KGC did not come from working in a courthouse. The blood of sentinels coursed through her veins.

"Are you saying Bessie *knew* Cowboy?"

"After Bessie's pa died, she took over for him. Oh, she didn't ride with Cowboy or anything, but he could count on her to get the word out to the Texas sentinels when needed. Her job at the courthouse made it easy. Cowboy trusted her, so I trust her."

*Do not underestimate Bessie,* I thought to myself. This tiny southern belle became a liaison for the KGC, and now she was the liaison for Granny and me. She *did* know all the secrets.

"What about Viva? Was she involved, too?" I asked. Each answer spawned two more questions.

"Lordy, no," Granny answered with a snort.

I heard disdain coupled with amusement in her voice. I wished I could see her face.

"Cowboy despised Viva. Didn't trust her any farther than he could throw her. She was always poking and prodding at Ora, trying to get her to tell her what Cowboy was up to. Viva thought he had the other half of the map. Cowboy made sure Ora knew nothing. And, to be truthful, Ora didn't care much to know. He provided for her and the kids. That was all she wanted."

*Wow.* Ora's husband hated her best friend. Yet, Ora had trusted Viva enough to give her the box with all of Cowboy's documents. How odd. Did Granny know Viva had that box in her possession? I believed not. "So, you don't trust Viva because of Cowboy?"

"I have my own reasons, missy, and they have to do with Darrell."

I cursed and praised the darkness in a single thought. I wanted desperately to see Granny's face, but I thanked all the powers that be that she could not see mine. What could my husband have done? I must know the truth.

"Go on," I said, struggling to contain my nerves.

"My boy and Darrell were good friends. Cowboy didn't approve because of Viva, but they were just boys, fourteen or fifteen years old. Darrell had nothing to do with Cowboy's qualms with Viva, so I let it be. They traipsed the woods at night with their ole Bluetick hounds, treeing coons or any other varmint that ran. You could hear the echoes of howling and barking through the valley until well after midnight. I didn't worry much about 'em. They both grew up shooting guns and chasing coons. The next morning, a pile of animal carcasses lay on the back porch, and two hungry boys sat on the stoop waiting for breakfast. They washed up while I cooked enough bacon and eggs to feed an army. They wolfed it down like it was their last meal here on earth," she said with a chuckle.

She recounted this memory with fondness. I could find no trace of dislike in her voice.

"One night, they didn't come home. About daylight, I took off looking for 'em. I tramped through those hills for hours, looking for my boy. I found him at the bottom of a rocky ravine, his head bashed in from a fall. He got hurt bad. Took two men to get him out of there. I didn't know for days if he would make it. He finally pulled out of it, but he never talked right again. I'm not sure he could think right either. He's not slow or retarded, but it's sure hard for him to get words out or into that head of his."

That explained it. This stoic man lacked the ability, not the desire, to communicate. I assumed Buddy to be hostile toward me, but he simply could not speak well.

Granny shifted in the rocker. I did not want her to stop here. I needed the rest of the story, so I nudged her on.

"Surely, Buddy's accident did not make you mad at Darrell."

"Missy, you need to listen very carefully to the words I don't say. Darrell and Buddy went out together. I found Buddy alone and injured. Why didn't Darrell stay with him? Why didn't he call for help?"

I had no answers for either question. Darrell's actions

defied the tenets of friendship. Equally disturbing, I did not catch the missing pieces of the puzzle. I heard what I wanted to hear, which excluded any references that might cast doubt on Darrell's behavior.

"When Buddy got better, he acted crazy. Kept asking for Cowboy. It was hard to make out, but he wanted Cowboy, all right. I fetched him, and he went into Buddy's room and closed the door. He spent a long time in there. When he left, he had a folded piece of paper in his shirt pocket. I asked him what Buddy wanted. All Cowboy said is, 'It's none of your concern. I'll take care of it.' Then he left. Darrell never came around again. The next day, an explosion blew a hole in the side of Sugar Loaf Mountain. You could hear the blast and the rumble of rocks tumbling down the ravine all over the valley, but none of us ever spoke about it. Not even a whisper."

Granny's voice had turned hoarse and raspy.

*Thunder nation, don't stop now*, I pleaded in my head. The rustling of Granny's clothes and a creak on the floor told me she rose from the rocker, ready to call it a night.

"Will you lead me to my room, missy?"

I felt my way to the other side, took Granny's hand, and began the slow shuffle down the hall. I helped her prepare for bed and then retraced my steps to the spare bedroom, which had become my temporary refuge. I had much to think about tonight.

# Chapter XVII

The first day of autumn made a respectable appearance dressed in a cool, blue sky. The sunlight pierced the small window in my room, taking a direct aim at my eyes. I sensed the morning hour to be late. Slipping out of bed, I made my way to the kitchen. No signs of Granny or Buddy. Instead, I found the nameless woman clearing the breakfast table.

"Good morning," I said tentatively.

After her huffy departure yesterday, I did not know what to expect. She paused mid-step, balancing a stack of dirty dishes precariously in one hand.

Her glance sized me up as if she didn't yet know what to make of me. "Hope you don't expect me to fix your breakfast. Everyone else done already ate."

I stood there, jaw dropped, blinking rapidly.

"No … No … of course not."

A plate of biscuits and a pot half full of coffee sat on the counter.

"I'll grab a couple biscuits and fill my tumbler with coffee," I said, moving around her. "I'm on my way out."

She scrunched up her face and scowled. "Suit yourself. Some of us have work to do."

I had work to do, too. Thoughts of Race Horse Creek had niggled at my brain until I surrendered. I knew Granny would not approve of my excursion, but I suspected secrets remained buried at the crest of the mountain. The outing would calm my fears and clear my head. I slipped on sturdy leather boots and jeans, ditching the flimsy sneakers and shorts I wore this morning.

It took only a few minutes by foot to get to the creek at the bottom of the hill. I retraced Bessie's route, arriving at the ledge with loosened rocks. Grabbing a sturdy stick, I poked and prodded at the rubble. The rocks yielded nothing except more rocks. How disappointing. What did I expect? Gold or diamonds to come tumbling out?

Not discouraged, I sat on a boulder and looked around for clues. Thirty yards down the bank, I noticed the bent trunk of a poplar pointing straight up the embankment. *Could this be a sign?* I lacked confidence after Bessie laughed about the scribblings on a rock, but I pressed on. One 'clue' after another led me to the top of a precipice overlooking the entire valley. The vigorous climb released my pent-up tensions, but my dog-tired legs needed a break. I lay back on a large rock to rest, soaking up the solitude of this wild terrain. My body took a break, but my mind continued to spin the clues in an endless circle.

My eyes darted to a covey of birds erupting from the tall grass. They cawed and flapped in a frenzy. I bolted upright, my heart pounding. I saw nothing else.

*Calm down*, I told myself. *It's just birds.*

Gathering my wits about me, I decided to leave. The biscuits had worn off, and my stomach growled. Stiffened from the rest, my legs needed a little coaxing. As I rose, noises rustled in the overgrown brush. Twigs snapped. *That's no bird,* I thought to myself.

The rustling grew louder. I cocked my head, listening. *Crack!* A broken tree limb? This thing had to be large ... very large.

I dropped to the ground and slid down the solid shoulder of the rock, moving as fast as I could without free falling. I planted my feet on a landing and took off running. I couldn't remember how to find the road. *Please, God, let me see a bent tree or a sign that I am on the right track.*

My legs pumped up and down, lifting the heavy leather boots with great effort. Round river rocks rolled under my feet, making it hard to keep my balance. I ran and ran, blood coursing through my beet-red face. Finally, the road. I did not stop or slow down until I reached Granny's shanty at the top of the hill.

Safely inside the house, my body quivered from head to toe. My imagination had veered out of control lately, but *someone* had been in those woods. Could it have been Darrell or Buddy or, God forbid, the man in the tan shirt?

I wanted to see Bessie. In bad situations, her wispy southern drawl and slow-moving words proved comforting. I could not risk a trip to Barber, but how I wished she was here. The triangulation of Granny, Bessie, and Viva puzzled me. I distrusted Viva from top to bottom. The jury remained out on Granny, but I found Bessie a strong ally.

I wandered out to the shade of the front porch and plopped down in Granny's rocker. The churning of my mind slowed down. The brightness of the autumn day helped me squash visions of the stalker in the woods. I needed to regain control.

The late morning sun washed the entire valley in a golden light. The dark green leaves of the poplars displayed tinges of yellow and orange. Fall would be in full force soon. The peaceful, bucolic hills buried the undercurrents of violence and poverty. This melancholy morning allowed the stories I had heard these last few months to crowd my thoughts.

The soft shuffling of Granny's feet interrupted my reverie. Her long, silver hair, twisted in a tight knot at the nape of her neck, emphasized the sharp angles of her face. A gauzy, flowered housecoat rippled gently about her small frame as it caught the morning breeze.

"Take this before I burn myself." Granny's hand trembled as she handed me a hot cup of coffee. "Beautiful, isn't it?" She settled into a chair.

I nodded, not wanting to disturb the peace of the morning.

"I sit out here a lot gathering my thoughts … just as I suspect you are doing."

I wished I could share all the thoughts my mind had gathered as I sat on the porch, but caution blocked the path.

"Enjoy your hike this morning?" she asked, tilting her head.

Busted. The only secrets in these hills were the ones kept from me. I did not answer.

"Kay, these hills are not safe. I thought you understood that."

"Yes, ma'am," I said, ducking my head in shame. Granny offered me refuge, and I returned defiance.

"Got scared, did you?" she giggled, eyes dancing with amusement. "Lordy, Buddy said you were scurrying down the hillside like a scared rabbit trying to outrun a coyote."

"Buddy? That was Buddy? Why didn't he call out? I wouldn't have run if I knew it ... " I stopped mid-sentence. Buddy could not 'call out.' He could barely speak. I quickly switched the topic to cover my blunder.

"Granny, where does it end? Can there ever be a happy ending?"

This mess had crossed several generations. I craved answers. I wanted to know if life contained only struggle and strife, heartache, and disappointment. The image of Ellie, Ora's mother, shelling peas in her apron as she waited for Ben Townsend to return, burned a hole in my heart. The need to provide for her children dictated her fate. Ora followed the footsteps of Ellie and married a man she did not know to escape dealing with life on her own. Viva, on the other hand, clung desperately to Darrell to fill the void left by her late husband. She needed a reason for being, even to the point of overlooking physical and mental abuse. And, poor Bessie carried the heartache of a widow as well as buried her only son. So much sorrow, and yet no room for self-pity.

"The business of living trumps all, missy. You need to remember that. My plight might seem hopeless and scary, but I will survive. So will you," she said with a nod.

Granny must have read my mind.

"You want me to tell you that life is different, harder, and meaner here than other places? Well, it's not. It's the same everywhere. Always has been ... always will be."

She seemed satisfied with her answer. Not me.

"I don't believe we have to accept what is given to us. Surely, we can fight for more." I refused to surrender my vision of peace and happiness on the other side of the windowpane.

Granny smiled as if I were an innocent child too naïve

to understand. "Life is the same all over, Kay. How we deal with life makes the difference. You see, there are two kinds of people in the world — those who drift with the current and end up where the river takes them and those who fight the currents until they reach their destination." She shrugged. "Either way, the water is the same. The river runs with the same undercurrents, muddy waters, eddies, and floods for all of us. The outcome is what's different. It just depends on which one you are."

"Which one was Ora … or Ellie, for that matter?"

"Ora and Ellie? Why, they were just drifters."

"Bessie and Viva?"

"Oh, Lordy," she said with a chuckle "Viva is definitely a pilot. Bessie … I'm not sure. I'm just not sure."

# Chapter XVIII

Buddy appeared after lunch with Bessie in tow. I could barely see her head above the dash of his '66 Chevy truck. Buddy helped her out, handing her the brocade box of letters before disappearing toward the barn. Bessie's spry steps made quick work of the path to the house, and Granny whisked us off to the parlor. I squeezed Bessie tight, clinging to her like a rag doll.

Granny waved her hands at us. "Enough of that," she said. "This is not a social visit. We need to help you, Kay."

We gathered our chairs in a snug circle around a small table. With great fanfare, Bessie placed her box in the center. When she opened the lid, I spied the familiar bundles separated by black ribbons.

"I marked the most important ones," Bessie informed us. She scooped the top bundle out of the box and spun toward me, placing her hand on my arm. "Dear, do you remember I told you that some think Darrell killed Kendra?"

*Remember? How could I forget?* She didn't wait for my answer.

"Well, I read through the rest of Viva's letters. Many of the letters troubled me. I think you will find them disturbing, too." A familiar grimace tugged at the corners of her mouth. Bessie loved drama.

"My memory is not what it used to be, but my logic is still good," she added, tapping a finger on her temple.

It seemed important to her that I remember her logic was 'still good.' She pulled the first letter from the sacred pile and began reading.

Dear Bessie,

Ora came by today. She hasn't come around in a long time. Cowboy doesn't approve of me, but I don't care much for him either. Seems he left her. She says they KIDNAPPED him! She won't admit it, but I think he tired of her and them kids. He went into Barber and never returned home. Ora is beside herself, worrying about how to provide for them kids. The oldest dropped out of school and took a job to make ends meet. All I can say is Ora gets to live hand-to-mouth like the rest of us now, and it's good enough for her. All those years of a free ride with Cowboy are over.

Like I said, I think Ora's lying about the kidnapping. Just the same, I am a little worried. Darrell took off over two months ago now. I haven't seen him since Cowboy disappeared. I hope he had nothing to do with it. Maybe he's a boy trying to be a man. I just don't know.

Enough rambling for now. Bessie, please don't tell anyone ANYTHING I have told you. I know I can trust you.

Write when you can.

Viva

Did Viva distrust her own son? Love and distrust make awful companions. I knew that to be a fact as I pondered my situation.

Bessie picked up the next letter and read again. She refused to share the duty with anyone.

Dear Bessie,

Hope this letter finds you well. Darrell hasn't straightened out. In fact, I think he's worse. He came home a couple months back and took to sneaking around at night again. I can't control him. He roamed the woods with Granny Snow's boy last Friday. He snuck off as usual and came home all scraped and bruised. I asked him what happened. I'm not sure I should tell you, but you are the only friend I got. It's not that I don't trust you, but if this ever got into the wrong hands it would be trouble for both of us.

He said they found the treasure everybody has been looking for. They drew a map so they could find it again and tore it in two. Each took a half and agreed to come back when they had a plan. Well, those two got into a fight — pushing and shoving like boys will do. Darrell said Buddy slipped and fell off the cliff into a deep ravine. Thought he might be dead. Darrell wanted to go back, but I said no. Maybe he wanted to find the other half of the map. I told him to sit tight. Keep his mouth shut. His life wouldn't be worth a plug nickel if those people thought he tried to hurt or kill Buddy. We didn't know for days if Buddy would live. He got hurt real bad.

I never will understand Darrell. He gets real hateful when I keep him from going out at night, but he just shrugged when I told him not to help Buddy. Anyhow, a mother can't be too careful. He's all I've got, you know.

I'll keep you posted. Bessie, please don't tell a soul about the map.

Until next time.

Viva

That Viva and Darrell abandoned Buddy in the ravine stunned me. I could see an immature boy following his mother's instructions, but Viva's own motherly instincts should have sent her flying to Buddy's side … or at least to Granny Snow. The blatant disregard for Buddy's life made my lunch turn sour until I had to fight back the bile. Granny told me she trusted neither of them. Now, I knew why. Did they act out of stupidity and fear, or could it have been self-serving?

Granny's face reflected my disgust, but her clenched jaw prevented words from escaping. Her brow, creased with tense furrows as Bessie read, relaxed. She bobbed her head up and down, completely understanding the events surrounding Buddy and Darrell.

Bessie, on the other hand, appeared deep in thought. I could almost hear the wheels turning. She knew more about this than what she read.

"What do you think? Was it an accident or deliberate?" I said.

"Be quiet, missy," Granny said. "There is more to the story."

Well, well, well, this felt familiar. It had been a while since one of my ladies rebuked me. I now lived hidden in a remote shanty flanked by two ancient souls of steel. No need to fly under the radar or play games. The truth gushed from Viva's own hand.

"Spell it out for me." My ultimatum hung in the air like the stench of dirty, wet socks.

Bessie nodded at Granny. "You tell her. It's your story."

The women stared at each other for several long moments. Finally, Granny cleared her throat.

"I need some water, Kay, and Minnie's not here. Would you fetch me some, please?"

I welcomed the short break. I made my way to the kitchen, returning with three glasses of water. As I handed Granny her drink, I noticed her face looked peaked.

"Are you okay?" I asked. "We can stop for a while."

She shook her head. "No. I want to keep going. We must deal with this, and I'm not getting any younger." She smiled, but I could see the pain hiding behind her peaceful façade.

The effect Viva's letter had on Granny worried me, but her determination remained strong. She took a few sips from the glass and placed it on the table.

"Now, I know what I suspected from the beginning."

She bent her head and rested her chin on her interlocked fingers. With her eyes closed, she looked as if she were praying. Granny took several deep breaths before returning her gaze to me.

"I'm gonna tell it to you plain and true. Darrell and Buddy prowled the woods at night pretending to coon hunt, but they were really treasure hunting. They combed those hills, night after night, searching for buried gold and jewels. The sentinels knew what they were up to, but they were just boys, so the sentinels paid them little mind. I didn't approve of Darrell, but I turned a blind eye as well." She shrugged. "The main problem was he was a Hacker … just like Viva."

I spewed water across the table. "Viva is a Hacker?"

"Yes, she is Ezra's younger cousin. She wasn't very old when Ezra got hung."

It had never crossed my mind Viva might have adopted Darrell because of blood kinship. She had told me a story dusted with generous portions of lies and omissions. She led me to believe she had helped a friend. Granny's choice of words about Ezra spun around in my head.

"What do you mean 'when Ezra got hung?' Didn't he hang himself?"

Granny shook her head. "I don't think so, missy. Ben Townsend, Ora's stepdad, was a sentinel and knew all about their inner workings. Ezra used Ora to eavesdrop, and she told him everything she knew. A simple woman, she just did as he asked. That's how Ezra got himself hung. A treasure hunter is no match for a sentinel."

Viva's words echoed in my head. "Kay, remember, the poem says Ora Price was the cause of it all. But think about that! When Ezra died, her name was *Hacker*, not Price, and no one knew that better than her husband. I can't think of any law — old or new — that would put a man in jail for wife abandonment. Yes, they found Ezra Hacker hanging in that jail, but he did not hang himself, and he did *not* write that poem."

So, the sentinels had murdered Ezra. I shivered with the realization that death came easy in the Ozarks.

"Did Cowboy kill him?"

"No, but he knew those who did. He came to Barber to head up the sentinels and then married Ora as a duty to another sentinel. Ben wanted a husband for Ora to replace the one they had killed."

It appeared the sentinels orchestrated Ezra's death. If so, Ora drifted with the current, swept along with the tide of another's purpose. Ben had a purpose. Ezra had a purpose. Cowboy had a purpose. And, yes, Viva had a purpose; she sought the other half of the map to the treasure on Sugar Loaf Mountain, true to her Hacker blood.

Granny shifted her weight before continuing. "Viva's pa came here to bury Ezra after the hanging. No one else would do it. The people around here shunned the Hacker family. Treated them like traitors. The Hackers became bitter people. That's why Joseph's family moved to California."

The love-hate relationship between Viva and Ora crystalized. Ora unknowingly had a hand in Ezra's death, and yet she had given Viva the gift of a son, Darrell.

Another question remained unanswered. "Then who wrote

the poem, and why?" I asked.

The poem condemned Ora to a lifetime of shame. There had to be a reason.

"Well, everyone knew that Ben Townsend only tolerated Ora for Ellie's sake. He always called her the 'Price' girl. If you remember, the poem called her 'Ora Price.' No one would take it down either. That poem lasted as long as the jail — a reminder to Ora that she had betrayed the sentinels. She never talked about Ben's business again for fear she would suffer the same fate."

Poor Ora. No wonder she had few friends and lived under the protection of Cowboy and the sentinels.

"Ahem," said Bessie.

Granny and I glanced up at her. With all these new discoveries, I had almost forgotten she sat around the table with us.

"You've gotten completely off track, Granny," Bessie admonished. "You were telling her about Darrell."

Granny clapped her hand over her mouth as if she had just belched in the middle of a church service. "Lordy, I almost forgot. Told you I can't keep my stories in a straight line. Now, where did I leave off?" Granny asked with a humorless laugh.

"Darrell and Buddy … the fight," Bessie prodded.

"Oh, yes. Viva's letter says they got in a scuffle. I believe Darrell wanted Buddy's half of the map, and he wouldn't give it to him. When Buddy walked away, Darrell must have shoved him off the edge of the ravine. It should have killed him." Granny paused and looked away. "I think he meant to."

I swallowed the lump in my throat. My husband tried to kill Buddy over a map, and Viva felt no remorse about covering it up as long as her son remained safe and out of trouble. The whole story made me sick to my stomach.

"What did Cowboy do?" I asked.

"I had no clue what paper Cowboy put in his pocket when he left Buddy's room, but now I am fairly certain it was Buddy's half of the map. They never told me about a map, but Viva did.

"Cowboy said the boys stumbled upon a cave with gold bricks stacked to the ceiling and jewels tumbling out of wooden chests. Buddy couldn't leave fast enough. He feared the KGC. Darrell wanted to stuff his pockets and come back for more. Cowboy took care of that, and he didn't need any map."

She puffed her chest up with pride. "The explosion on Sugar Loaf Mountain sealed the entrance to the cave forever."

My mind reeled. The wealth of the KGC existed in the bowels of Sugar Loaf Mountain, and my husband had a portion of the map marking the location. Darrell never shared this with me, and Viva had not uttered a peep.

Granny took a sip of water. "Things came up missing after Ora died. One was a box she kept all her papers in after Cowboy passed. I always suspected Viva took it. From what I heard today, she probably wanted the map; but I can't prove it."

So, Viva's story about Ora's boys was a lie. I had never believed Viva worried over Ora's children. She wanted Buddy's map. The thought of my mother-in-law stealing from her best friend boggled my mind. *Who would ever do such a thing?*

Bessie and I glanced at each other across the table. Viva had changed all right, more than either of us suspected. She had morphed into a treasure hunter and a thief. Granny's suspicions about the box were correct, but fear silenced our tongues.

"I'll finish," Bessie murmured, obviously impatient to move on. "Viva is lying to me in her letters and lying to herself, too."

Such strong words from Bessie caught me off guard.

"They kidnapped Cowboy. And, she knew it! Every sentinel from Arkansas to Texas looked for him. Whoever took him must have been sharp, because we couldn't find any trace of him."

The word 'we' struck a chord. This petite southern charmer had played a role in the search for Cowboy. I didn't want to ask the next question, but I had no choice.

"Did Darrell kidnap Cowboy?" I hoped the answer would be no.

Bessie snickered. "Darrell wasn't that cagey, but I think he had a hand in it. We spotted him down in Texas, near Granbury, several times."

My *loving* husband not only tried to kill Buddy, but he also helped kidnap Cowboy. At this point, I felt no sense of surprise. The man I thought I had married did not exist.

"They were treasure hunters. They knew Cowboy could lead them to all the gold," said Bessie. "They didn't know Cowboy would never tell. They tortured him for almost a year, but he never revealed a word."

"Did the sentinels ever find him?"

"No, but he escaped. Ora got a letter from Texas two days after Cowboy got home. Said they held him in the town where John Wilkes Booth hid, and those people would never bother anyone again."

Even I understood what Cowboy meant, but I did not understand the John Wilkes Booth reference.

"John Wilkes Booth? How does he play into all this?" I asked.

"Don't let that concern you now, dear. Another time," Bessie said, dismissing me with a flick of her wrist. "Right now, we need to worry about you."

My head spun with the flood of information I learned

this afternoon, yet I still knew nothing about Kendra's death. My forebodings about Darrell ran deep, and I would believe anything Bessie or Granny said about him. They had planted the seeds of doubt with the stories of Viva, Buddy, and Cowboy. Somehow, my life intertwined with Kendra's death. I just needed the truth.

I reached across the table and clasped Granny's arm. "Then, Kendra. Tell me about Kendra," I pleaded.

"It's time," said Granny. "You need to know." She nodded as if trying to convince herself. "Kendra was my granddaughter, Skeeter's oldest girl. Long, reddish-blonde hair, hazel eyes … tall and slender like a willow. Oh, my, how I loved that little girl."

Granny smiled as she reflected on her memories, eyes glistening with tears.

Lights went off in my head. That would make Skeeter and Buddy brothers, and Darrell would be Skeeter's son-in-law. Skeeter must hate Darrell. Did he marry Kendra to get his hands on the map? I shivered with the realization that my refuge might be a cesspool of bad blood.

"She was as strong-minded as she was sweet, and she was certainly nobody's fool," Granny said with a note of defiance.

I had always been a little jealous of Kendra, but as I listened, I felt an affection for this strong, beautiful young woman. My emotions twisted like a pretzel.

"She and Darrell got close when he and Buddy were running the woods. She tagged along with them sometimes. Knew her way around better than the both of them. I don't think there was a place in these hills she didn't know. She got sentinel blood from her pa," Granny said, her face glowing with pride. "He took her with him ever since she was a tadpole. I didn't like it, but he did it anyway."

"Didn't Buddy's incident cause a rift?"

"Yes, but between her and her family, not her and Darrell. He told her it was an accident. She believed him. I tried to talk sense into her, but I had no proof, and I didn't know about the map until today. The map might have made a difference. I don't know."

I glimpsed a remorseful Bessie out of the corner of my eye. This day gave all of us a bitter pill to swallow. If Granny had known of the map revealed in Viva's letters, Kendra might have believed her story about Darrell and Buddy. The bottom of Bessie's rose and ivy brocade box might have harbored Kendra's salvation.

"Didn't Buddy tell her?"

Granny shook her head. "He stayed to himself after the accident. Anyway, Darrell could be charming if he had a mind to."

I could not argue with that. He had captured my heart quickly with his easy-going manner and laugh.

"And, Darrell picked *her* to charm. Especially after Buddy's fall. I suspect now he wanted to use her like Ezra had used Ora — to get at the treasure."

"What happened then?" I asked.

"They married right after Cowboy's kidnapping. Darrell wasn't welcome in my home, so Kendra wouldn't come either. We lived in the same county, but I didn't see her for nearly a year.

"Then, one day, she showed up on my doorstep." Granny's brow furrowed. "My little sunshine girl looked down and out. She asked me to tell her what had happened to Buddy again. I don't know why. She already knew what I would say. But, I repeated it for her. This time I think she listened. Anyway, she didn't stay long. That was the last time I saw my baby girl."

Granny fell quiet. Her eyes puddled with tears. My own eyes grew misty, watching her struggle with the emptiness of grief.

Granny wiped her eyes with her apron.

"How did Kendra die?" I asked as gently as I could.

"Snakebite."

Copperheads and timber rattlers! I hated snakes, and they seemed to be under every rock in the Ozarks.

"How awful." I shuddered. "They are everywhere. I watch my step every time I go outside."

"Not outside, missy. In her bed."

My mouth dropped open. *How would a snake wind up in her bed?*

"Darrell had trapped copperheads and kept them in a pit in the backyard for the Snake Festival. It's a big sport around these parts. Lots of crazy fools spend their summers trapping those vipers. Darrell claimed he didn't know how one got into the house and in her bed, but no one believed him." Granny rolled her eyes. "I don't think even Viva believed him. Anyway, I couldn't prove it. A slick way to commit murder, if you ask me."

My skinned crawled. Murder by venom would be hard to prove.

"Darrell doesn't keep snakes now," I said. "Or does he?" I mumbled under my breath.

Now, that I knew Kendra's story, I couldn't understand Viva's comment about our similarities.

"Why did Viva say I am like Kendra?" I asked my ladies. "I am not the daughter of a sentinel. I know nothing about treasures." I gripped my water glass tighter as my anxiety rose.

"I think I know why," said Bessie. "He *chose* you, just like he *chose* Kendra."

"But, I am nothing like her," I cried.

"More than you think, dear." Bessie smiled. "More than you think."

I could not comprehend what a beautiful mountain girl like Kendra could have in common with a nerdy professor of chemistry. She grew up in these rugged Arkansas hills. I knew only the bricks and concrete of Little Rock.

"How are we alike?" I slammed my glass down on the table, sloshing water onto the table.

"Missy, you're nothing alike in looks *or* temperament, I might add," Granny said, glancing at the puddle on the table. "She knew the secrets of the KGC Darrell wanted so badly. He underestimated her loyalty. When she refused to tell him, he turned on her. That's when she came to see me."

Granny's lips drooped into a frown. "I could see the fear in her eyes, but that girl was too independent to let me help. She said she had gotten herself into this mess, and she would get herself out."

"None of that has anything to do with me. I know nothing," I said.

"It wasn't what you knew, Kay. He needed your brains, your drive to solve puzzles. And, didn't Viva send you up here to meet me?"

*Yes, but Bessie did, too,* I thought.

My mind replayed the first time I met Darrell. *I shared your research with Darrell, Kay. Hope you don't mind.* I had just finished two years on research for the treatment of diabetes. *The Journal of Analytical Chemistry* had published my finding, offering generous praise for my problem-solving abilities. Mark implied they had discussed my research at length, but Darrell never mentioned it to me. How ironic that the sterile, detached world of science became the siren call for buried treasure.

"But, Darrell told me to stay away from Cowboy and Texas and, and, everything." My thoughts ran topsy-turvy through my mind, and I couldn't make sense of it all. "Why did he do that? He was mad at me for getting involved."

"Do you really think Viva would go to Texas with you if Darrell disapproved?" Granny drilled a finger into the table. "Viva and Darrell knew exactly what they were doing. If you suspected what they were up to, you never would have stayed, missy."

"So, I am like Kendra because Darrell wanted to use both of us? Is that it?"

"Yes," said Bessie, "You are also like Kendra because you questioned Darrell. Remember, dear, you asked Viva why Granny didn't trust the two of them. That was Viva's breaking point. She knew then you'd be of no use to her."

Yes, I remembered. I wanted to test their mettle, just as Granny had tested mine. Instead, I provided Viva with the only truth she needed. My doubts marked me as a traitor. The illusion of flying under the radar evaporated. Viva sized me up pretty well. She sensed a shift in loyalty and no longer needed my help. Kendra and I did have a lot in common. We refused to surrender to their will.

I sighed. How could I be so foolish? "What did they want from me?"

"The other half of the map, dear. They think Granny has it," Bessie said.

"Cowboy took the map."

"I didn't even know there *was* a map until today," said Granny. "I surely don't have it."

She hid a map in that black purse she carried the day we

had ice cream. Why would Granny lie? Back under the radar.

The evening shade crept across the front porch, threatening darkness soon. Granny edged up from her chair and stood for a minute, letting her stiffened legs regain their strength. Bessie bounded to her feet, none the worse for wear.

"Are you ladies hungry?" Granny said, breaking the intensity of the evening. "I think I've got some leftovers. I told Minnie I wouldn't need her for a few days, so we are on our own."

"Doesn't Viva expect you, Bessie?" I asked.

She shook her head. "Not for a while. I told her I needed to go back to Texas to tend to some business. She took me to the bus herself. I had Buddy pick me up in Booneville, and I came straight here. I guess you and I are Granny's guests or prisoners, depending on how you want to look at it," she added with a chuckle.

Bessie seemed to relish our predicament, a sentiment I did not share. My instincts refused to trust her easy manner. I had no stomach for a late-night talk in a dark parlor. I retired early, leaving my cohorts to go it alone.

A flood of paranoia washed over me. I knew Granny had a map that never left her side, yet she claimed to know nothing. It appeared Darrell and Viva had the other half, but without both halves, the map was useless. Kendra would not share the location of the treasure, a secret that led to her death. Bessie exhibited a cavalier attitude in the presence of danger, but maybe *her* danger was not real. As I sifted through my thoughts, one thing became clear: Bessie's allegiance lay with the sentinels. Her loyalty shifted from Viva to me the minute Granny took me into her confidence. Had Viva and Darrell played me with Bessie's help, or had I become the conduit for Bessie to get to Granny? I could trust no one. I made plans to leave in the morning, taking Granny's map and the letters in Bessie's box with me.

Rising before daybreak, I tiptoed into Granny's room and gently slipped the map from the black purse hanging by the door. Then I snuck into Bessie's room. This proved to be harder. The box, pushed under the bed, lay right below Bessie's pillow. Her rhythmic snoring gave me the courage to slide on my belly to the edge of the bed and take her prized box.

My heart pounded as I raced back to my room. Buddy could return home anytime. He moved in and out of the house like a ghost all times of night and day. Thankfully, no Buddy appeared. I donned my boots, as thoughts of snakes danced in my head, before making my way down the hall and out the door to … what? To safety? Safety did not exist in the shadow of the Sugar Loaf Mountain.

An hour of hard hiking brought me to a crossroads. Left would take me to Magazine and right to Booneville. Magazine seemed the better choice. The sleepy little town did not have a bus station, but I could pay the driver and get on. My feet had blistered from the boots long before I reached my destination, but I kept moving. Finally, I saw the outline of buildings on the horizon. I made it. Before long, a silver bus pulled up to the corner. I boarded and made my way to the back. Sleep and a greyhound bus would get me to Memphis quickly.

# Chapter XIX

The Memphis-Arkansas Memorial Bridge, spanning the river, offered an expansive view of the banks of the Mississippi. Warehouses and docks lined the murky waters that teamed with barges and boats transporting goods up and down the massive waterway. The hustle and bustle of the highway seemed out of place with the lazy drift of tug boats pushing and pulling cargo. Memphis pushed the tiny town of Barber off the face of the earth, and I did not miss it. The homeless and panhandlers crowded the bus station lobby, so I did not linger. After walking several blocks, seedy surroundings gave way to urban renewal of the downtown entertainment district. Weekly rentals abounded in this neighborhood. I took the first available one.

*Safe at last*, I thought, *safe at last*. I threw my belongings at the foot of the bed and climbed beneath the sheets for much-needed rest.

The daylight clamor of the streets below jarred me from a deep, deep sleep. My eyes focused on a brown water stain on the ceiling sliding down to a window framed with filthy chintz curtains. A blue chair, a small desk, and a well-used chest of drawers furnished the small room. I took a moment to remember what had brought me to this barren little room in Memphis. I strolled to the window and peered down at a narrow street lined with parked cars glistening with the drizzle of early morning rain. Passersby streamed up and down the sidewalk, trailing in and out of small eateries and shops like an army of ants. My stomach growled. Food and a cup of coffee sounded wonderful. Scrambling down the stairs, I hastened to join the ant army.

The sweet aroma of homemade bread and hot coffee drifted into the streets from a deli just around the corner. I loaded up, with no intention of venturing out again. The mystery had engulfed my life since I had arrived in Barber, and today I would sort it out. A smile crossed my lips. No one would suspect that I, the nerd, would have the gumption to steal their secrets and run off to Tennessee. I headed back to my room, prepared to straighten this mess out.

Worn wooden steps groaned as I made my way up the dark stairwell. I shifted the groceries in my hands to turn the doorknob and pushed the rain-swollen door open with my back.

"What are you doing here, Kay?"

Startled, I dropped the bags. Darrell's voice came from the blue chair nestled close to the window. My eyes adjusted slowly to the dinginess of the room. His features looked haggard, emphasized by poor lighting. Bloodshot eyes peered at me from the shadow of a cap pulled low on his forehead. The toe of a muddy boot rested on the edge of Bessie's box, still sitting at the foot of the bed.

*How did you find me?* I shouted in my mind, but no words left my mouth.

Darrell's hand reached up and patted his vest pocket. "I have two tickets to Magazine. We are getting on the bus this afternoon."

Bus tickets? Darrell had a truck. Why did he have bus tickets?

I sized up my situation. Darrell's hunting jacket and vest concealed compartments for knives and ammo, much like a backwoodsman from the hills of Arkansas. Nothing about his attire suggested a friendly bus trip back to Magazine. Fear clutched my throat, choking out any utterance I tried to make. My silence seemed to agitate him. His hands moved from his jeans pocket to his face and back to his pockets again. He stood and paced the tiny room. I inched toward the door, hoping to make a run once Darrell turned away. Quick as a bolt of lightning, his arm shot above my shoulder and slammed the door behind me. *Trapped.*

"What is the matter with you?" he said with a tremor in his voice.

I had no choice but to fight.

"I know all about you, Darrell. I know all about Kendra and Buddy and … and … Cowboy. I know what you did, and I know why you did it," I shouted, carefully omitting any reference to the treasure map. I shifted about the room, staying as far away from him as possible.

"You know nothing! That's the problem. You *think* you know." Darrell dropped into the blue chair and slouched back, resting his head against the time-stained upholstery. He stared out the window for a moment before facing me again.

"You have all the answers, don't you? I've never met anyone as smart as you think you are." The corners of his mouth turned upward, feigning a smile.

His sarcasm made my eyes well up with tears. This crazed stranger in my room, a vestige of the man I loved. He crushed me. I hated crying because tears made me feel weak. I needed to regain my wits. *Think, Kay. Think.*

I could not physically escape, so I had to fight my way out with words. Logic and words had always been my choice of weapons.

"You tried to kill Buddy," I snarled. "You shoved him off a cliff and left him to die."

Darrell scrunched up his face as if I had punched in the stomach with all my might. The loud ticking of a clock exaggerated the oppressive silence. After heaving a sigh, he met my eyes once again.

"I don't know who told you that, but it's a lie," he said.

His voice held no emotion. He could have been talking about the weather. It felt like sparring with a rag doll. I pushed again to get the truth flowing.

"Granny told me, and your mother knew it, too." I spat the words at him, daring him to tell the truth.

"Do you *really* want to know what happened, Kay, or are you going to wrap it all up in one of your *logical* conclusions?" He thrummed his four fingers over and over on the chair arm as he awaited my answer.

"Yes, tell me the *truth*," I said, keeping up my guard. It would take a lot to convince me he had not tried to kill Buddy.

"Granny probably told you Buddy and I found the large cave filled with KGC treasure. We were just boys, too young to know what to do with our discovery. It was magnificent, Kay. Gold bars stacked ceiling high and chests filled with jewels everywhere. More wealth than either of us would ever see in a lifetime. Buddy said we should draw a map, each take half, and come back later."

Darrell shook his head, reveling in the memory of their unbelievable good fortune. "Can you imagine what would go through the minds of two nineteen-year-old boys thinking about that cave? Buddy said it belonged to the KGC, and we should tell Cowboy.

I laid awake that night thinking about what Mom could do with the money. Not all of it, just enough to get by without having to walk five miles every day to work or spend hours planting and canning so we could eat. You know, the KGC always took care of the sentinels. I wouldn't say they had a lot, but Granny and Ora had all they needed. Mom and I did without. I guess I thought the KGC could spare a little, so I told Buddy I planned to take some with me."

In my mind, I tried to reconcile the sin of stealing stolen gold. One boy wanted to ease the burden of his mom's hardscrabble existence, and the other wanted to protect the sentinels. Neither choice seemed evil.

"Go on," I said, mimicking the steeliness of Darrell's tone.

"We tussled over it. Buddy slipped and fell down the ravine. It scared me. Thought he was dead. I ran home as fast as I could and told Mom that Buddy needed help. She panicked. Mom locked the doors and told me to stay put. She feared they would blame me, and I would end up dead, too. They hung Grandpa Ezra for less."

Viva's letter called Buddy's fall an accident, and she feared for her own boy's safety if no one believed him. Buddy said Darrell tried to kill him, but Buddy was not right in the head. *Room for doubt? Maybe.*

"Let's go," Darrell said, signaling the conversation had ended.

"I'm not going anywhere with you until I get all the answers." My voice sounded filled with conviction. My insides, however, shook like a house near the tracks when a train rolls by.

"*All* of the answers, Kay. Where do you go to get *all* the answers?" That smirk curled his lips again.

His words burned with the acid of resentment that extended well beyond me. With his body hugging the chair and his head tilted back, he gazed at me, his half-closed eyes filled with disdain. The man and his past wrestled with the conversation, and I did not exist.

"What about Cowboy's kidnapping? Did you have a hand in that?"

"Let me guess. Granny again?"

"No, Bessie."

"Well, if Bessie said it, it must be true. Right?"

"I didn't say that."

"You didn't have to. I can see it in your face. Let me tell you about Bessie. She's a sweet old lady who has lost everything important to her. Her husband, her son, and her beloved south are all gone. She clung to Mom, reliving the past as if it were a current event. I don't know what she told you, but whatever it is, don't believe it. Be careful where you place your trust, Kay. You're smarter than that."

I crossed my arms across my chest. "I don't think she lied to me. Bessie's dad was a sentinel who rode with Cowboy. I think she is trying to protect me."

Darrell's tone softened. "If she told you I helped kidnap Cowboy, she would be wrong. Cowboy was the only father I knew. She may try to protect you, but make no mistake, Kay, her devotion to the KGC and the sentinels comes first. She abandoned Mom when she found out she hunted the treasure. I never wanted that to happen. Their friendship was the one true thing I did not want spoiled by this never-ending mess of greed and violence. Distance had preserved their bond until you brought them together."

Bessie never said Darrell kidnapped Cowboy. She only said they had seen him around Granbury. She had abandoned Viva, although I could not be sure of when. Her alliance shifted to me and, finally, to Granny as the truth about the maps unraveled. Suspicions and facts twisted together in my mind, and I failed to sort them out properly. Had I been swept away in this dust of lies?

"Are you a sentinel for the KGC?"

Darrell burst out in a belly laugh, growing red-faced and watery-eyed. It took several minutes for him to regain composure.

"Are you kidding? A Hacker?" he said as the laughter roiled up again. "Hackers weren't good enough for the KGC. Remember, they hung my grandpa, and I tried to steal their treasure. Even Ora didn't want her own grandson in the house, and Granny disowned her granddaughter because she married me."

"No, Kay, I am not a sentinel," he said soberly. "Nor do I want to be," he finished in a whisper. "The sentinels hate the treasure hunters, and the treasure hunters fear the sentinels. They are warring camps; at cross-purposes if you will. Grandpa Ezra lost his life in that war. Mom crossed the line when I brought her the map."

I did a quiet tally in my mind. Ezra and Viva sought the lost treasure. Cowboy, Granny, Skeeter, Buddy, Kendra, and

Bessie guarded the precious wealth of the KGC. Each camp possessed one half of the same map. *Did Darrell reject both?*

And what about Kendra? A marriage that defied the warring factions invited tragedy. I dreaded bringing this up, but why stop now? As long as he talked, I did not fear him.

"You have never told me how Kendra died." I purposely omitted Granny's story. I could not take more hateful rhetoric from Darrell.

"That's what is really bothering you, isn't it? Kendra torments your soul," he said with a sneer.

"She doesn't *torment* my soul!" I slurred the word torment, making it sound ugly in tone and context. Maybe Kendra tormented my soul, but not because she died. Images of the tall, slender girl with hazel eyes haunted me. Jealousy of a dead woman shamed me, but I could not control it. However, I now excelled in the art of lying.

"How did Kendra die?" I bellowed, losing control of my emotions.

"I will tell you, but it won't make a difference."

"What do you mean it won't make a difference? I don't understand you at all."

"That's the first true thing you've said today. Let's see if my story meets Granny's test. Kendra and I both loved snake hunting, so we did it for sport. Every year we trapped the biggest son of a gun we could find to enter the Snake Festival in the next county and threw them in a pit in the backyard. That year we caught a huge copperhead, but the pit wasn't deep enough, and it crawled out. Kendra grabbed a shovel and chopped his head off. Remember, Kay, that's what you do with snakes. You sever their heads."

Darrell's biting words dripped with bitterness.

"Our dogs smelled blood and excitement and came running. Afraid it would hurt one of the pups, she reached down and picked it up to sling it over the fence."

Darrell stopped talking and looked down at the floor.

"Did you know that dead snakes can still bite, Kay? Yep, even when they're dead, they writhe and squirm and spew poison. Like many people, I know." He nodded his head in an exaggerated motion.

*Could he be referring to Cowboy or Ezra?*

"It sunk its fangs into her left forearm, you know, the one closest to the heart. It struck several times, and I couldn't get help fast enough. Now, you know how Kendra died. End of story," he said with an expansive spread of his hands.

Snake venom paralyzes the respiratory muscles, causing death by suffocation. Few people die of a snake bite, but if it gets you enough times and in the right spot, it is fatal. What a horrible way to die.

The coldness of his manner struck me as unusual. Was he indifferent or numb to the tragedy of Kendra's death? Finally, I knew how his precious lady had died … if he was telling the truth.

This all started with a poem and ended with a web of deception and lies. I still did not know who or what to believe. What about Cowboy? Could he be a ghost conjured up to meet the emotional needs of three old women? I must know.

"Was Cowboy real?" I asked.

"Perhaps Cowboy was the only *real* thing in this whole mess," Darrell answered deliberately and without guile. "I got to know Cowboy while growing up. The man spoke in riddles, but he always told the truth. That's a rare commodity in these parts. It was up to you to figure out what he was saying.

'You need to understand, Cowboy had a mission, a purpose that surpassed the day-to-day struggles of being a hill farmer or moonshiner. As lead sentinel, all the treasurers of the KGC answered to him. He took care of Ora and the kids out of duty, but he would kill to protect the legacy of his father, Jesse Woodson James.'

'Those who didn't know him thought he was mean and heartless or killed for blood sport, but he only did what he had to do." Darrell stopped talking and shifted the cap on his head. He clasped his hands together and leaned forward as if to share a confidence.

"Pay attention if you want to know the measure of the man. I was headed for serious trouble when Buddy and I ran together. But, I wasn't a killer, and Cowboy knew that. Don't you think he would have killed me if he thought I had tried to murder Buddy? He cornered me after Buddy's accident and told me to listen up. His words still echo in my mind: 'If you ever kill a man, he will dance on your bedpost at night and follow you to your grave.' No riddle there. He knew exactly what he was talking about.

"You solved a lot of Cowboy's riddles, didn't you?" Darrell continued. "You should know better than anyone that Cowboy existed."

He drew a deep breath and exhaled slowly.

"You followed the trail and solved the riddles to prove who Cowboy really was. But, what did you gain? Here you are asking me to tell you what you already know but can't get your brain around. Even your smart little brain struggles with the mystery of Cowboy." He rubbed the back of his neck. "Kay, you are in grave danger."

My hand shot up to my bruised face. I winced as I touched the swollen skin.

"Your *friend* did this to me." The acid words shot from my mouth.

"He's no friend of mine. Quite the opposite, really. He's a treasure hunter searching for the other half of the map."

My mind jumped into overdrive. According to Viva's letters, she took Darrell's half of the map. According to Granny, Cowboy had the other half. Time to quiz him.

"Who has the maps?" I would know if he told the truth.

"You do. It's all in your hands."

His words sent me twirling. How did he know I had Granny's map?

"I only have Granny's map, Darrell." I planted my hands on my hips. "How on earth did you know?"

He rolled his eyes as if I asked the stupidest question in the world. "Do you think you could steal half of a treasure map, and no one would notice? You didn't think Skeeter or Buddy would know you and the map disappeared at the same time? And, Kay, you have both halves," he said again.

I feared they would know who took it, but I felt I had picked a safe hiding place in Memphis where no one could find me. *And*, I did not have the other map.

"I don't know what you are talking about."

Darrell bent over and picked up the file folder on the floor labeled 'Kendra.' He removed a piece of paper that looked like the other half of Granny's map and handed it to me. My hands trembled as I placed Granny's half next to it. A perfect match. *I* had the map to the KGC treasure of Sugar Loaf Mountain.

"That's what my *friend* was looking for when he showed

up at the house, and that's why you are in danger. I've kept that map out of the hands of treasure hunters for years, but the cat is out of the bag now, thanks to you."

"You mean from Skeeter and Buddy?"

"No, I am speaking about my *friend*. He came to the house searching for the map when he ran into you, and I can assure you he's been back and knows you took the file. I'm only here to help you. You're in way over your head."

"If he knew it was there, why did he wait so long to steal it?"

"He's a new one. I took care of the others before him?"

I shuddered to think about what that meant.

"Did you ever see lights in the woods at night?" He paused, waiting for an answer. I could only nod. "Well, that was my *friend* casing the house. He thought Mom hid the map, but I took it from her long ago."

"You left us alone with that madman skulking around the house!"

"Did I, Kay? I was never far away. I always had you in my sight. I kept close tabs on you."

"Why didn't you tell me?" I started to add he could trust me but stopped short.

"I didn't want to scare you. I only wanted to protect you. When you asked Mom why Granny did not trust me, I felt crushed. Granny never got over the loss of Kendra. Grief settles deeper into a woman's soul. Skeeter and Buddy knew the truth, but she couldn't shake the bitterness."

"Are Skeeter and Buddy a threat to me?"

"Maybe. I can't be sure. They trusted you, and you betrayed them. I do know you can't outrun them if they plan to come after you. Mostly, they're only concerned with guarding the treasures of the KGC. You need to go back and make amends."

*What had I done?* I wanted to believe Darrell, but my shot nerves wouldn't allow me to think. I sat in a stupor listening to the ticking clock.

Darrell became more restless the longer he waited for my response. He finally broke the silence. "Best I can tell, you don't need people much. You don't trust me, and you don't need my help. You just need a puzzle, a challenge, or a chance to prove how brilliantly you can solve any problem. So, I'm gonna leave you to it." He turned to go. "And, for the record, I am not a treasure hunter."

"If you are not a treasure hunter, why didn't you give your half of the map to the sentinels?"

He shrugged. "I probably should have, but I couldn't bring myself to betray Grandpa Ezra. He gave his life for the treasure. I felt like I owed him something. Twisted, isn't it?"

Darrell rose from the chair and strode from the room, slamming the door behind him.

He was wrong. I needed people more than I wished to admit, but I had spent my life failing to connect to anyone. *Could I break the pattern?* Books, work, research, and puzzles shielded me from personal interactions. I wanted to please Viva but had only incurred her anger. My quest to solve the mystery of Cowboy for Darrell unearthed answers to questions he never wanted asked. I had to find my way out of this sea of doubt. I turned back to the only method that had ever worked for me, my training in science. Who or what did I believe?

I must deal with one variable at a time and isolate each aspect of the puzzle before I could put the pieces together. I started with Bessie. I sat the brocade box on the bed and opened it. Each letter had been carefully placed, one on top of the other, by date.

The orderly ensemble soothed me. Oh, how I wished I could see Bessie's replies, but I would just have to read between the lines. I continued through the stack until I reached the bottom. The last letter in a pile dated back to a much earlier time. Bessie had one letter out of order, screwing up an otherwise perfect sequence of envelopes. I removed the contents and began to read.

Dear Bessie,

Well, things have settled down here. Darrell must have got drunk for the first time at the dance. Made him a little crazy. Anyway, he slept if off. When he woke up, he was so sheepish and fell all over himself, trying to get back in my good graces. I didn't let him off the hook easy. Some men get mean when they get drunk. He's one of 'em. I told him there would be no more drinking as long as he lived under my roof.

Garden's coming in so I have lots of canning to do. Wish you were here to help me. Ha! It's hard work, but sure will taste good this winter.

Write when you can.

Viva

This letter explained the tussle between Viva and Darrell but had never reached my eyes. My hands dropped to my lap.

All of my life, I felt excluded, somehow separated from life by a windowpane that only allowed me to peer at the other side where happiness and love resided. Other times, the pane trapped me on the inside. Buried deep in my need to excel or prove my worth, I could only look inward at the demons of my drive to succeed. I created both windows. Darrell almost had it right. I needed people, but I tried *not* to need them. The result was the same. These panes of glass existed only in my head.

This realization sent a wave of relief through my body. I needed Darrell, and I believed he needed me. He came to Memphis to protect me. He wanted me to help him heal the taint of hurt and violence that had begun with Ezra and followed his father, Joseph. I let myself get caught up in an age-old mystery and the vivid imaginations of three old ladies. The complexity of human emotions tested me, but I had to try. I would return to Barber and make atonement with Granny.

I took the first bus headed to Magazine the next morning. The hum of wheels on the highway carried my thoughts through the events of the last few months. Granny had said Darrell did not travel the river. The strangeness of her words played over and over like a broken record. The river had meaning. The common thread of KGC treasure bound my ladies together.

*That's it!* The pursuit of KGC gold *mus*t be the river. Ora and Ellie drifted. Bessie, Granny, and Viva navigated, always seeking to possess or protect both pieces of the map. *Darrell did not travel the river.* He was not a treasure hunter. The pieces began to fit. I could not wait to get home and share this with my husband. *People puzzles were not so hard*, I thought.

# Chapter XX

My anticipation of seeing Darrell made the trip to Magazine feel like a lifetime as the bus twisted and turned along the narrow Ozark highways. Finally, the silhouette of tiny brick stores and houses appeared in the distance. I dreaded the walk back to Barber, but I wanted to surprise him.

The bus pulled up in front of the Palace drugstore and dropped me on the corner with all my belongings. I slid my knapsack over my shoulders and grabbed the rest of the bags. Ready to hit the road, I saw Darrell's white truck parked catty-corner from the drugstore on a side street. *Was Darrell here? He wasn't expecting me.*

I lugged my heavy belongings across the road and threw them into the pickup bed. The brocade box, the map, and the files I had taken from Darrell's office I put in the front so they would not blow away. I hung around for him to finish whatever business had brought him to Magazine.

As I slid into the cab on the passenger side, I noticed the keys dangling in the ignition. The interior, usually littered with papers and used coffee cups, showed no trace of clutter. Someone had waxed the dash and leather seats to a high shine. The inside smelled of cleaning fluids. *Was this Darrell's truck? It had to be. I had given him a key ring with the letter 'D' engraved on it.*

The small town of Magazine had too many prying eyes to make my presence known. I just sat tight. Minutes turned into hours as I waited for his return, growing impatient with every passing second. I shrugged. Maybe he had caught a ride home. The truck started without a problem, so my theory of engine trouble disintegrated. I drove out of town, taking the long way around by the lake. I planned to stop by Granny's and return the map. I felt like a thief and needed to fix that situation.

The lake road allowed me to relax and enjoy the beautiful mountains. Brilliant orange and red foliage lit up the trees like a flameless fire. I felt my anxiety slip away into the shadows of the forest floor. No more chasing Cowboy and his sentinels for me.

Topping Sugar Loaf Mountain, I shifted into low gear for the steep descent to Granny's house. In the distance, I saw several cars parked at the bottom of the holler, just on the other side of Granny's. I pulled over, not wanting to get caught up in any brouhaha. Through Darrell's binoculars, I saw a rope of yellow police tape strung across the bridge. Two large men, one wearing a tan shirt and tie, appeared carrying a black bag about the size of a man. They picked their way down the side of the bluff, then along the stream's bed before emerging on the left bank of Race Horse Creek. They approached an ambulance and placed the bag in the rear compartment. The ambulance pulled away with no urgency, red light swirling in a slow and steady pace, headed toward Barber. One by one, the remaining cars left, following the ambulance like a funeral procession.

*A body bag? Someone died?*

The reporter in me resurfaced. The sun hung low in the sky, but I had enough time before sundown to check it out for myself. Still in my walking boots, I retraced the path I had traveled several times, looking for clues.

*Did someone fall ... maybe Buddy?*

Not sure I would recognize the site, I kept climbing anyway. Soon I reached the top of the bluff, the same bluff I had visited recently. When I came upon the clearing at the top of the mountain, I saw a short rope swinging from a poplar branch about seven feet off the ground. A hangman's noose dangled at the end of the rope, sliced in two to free its victim. Smooth river rock, once in a pile, had slid to the left like a waterfall, sending a flat sandstone slab to the bottom of the heap. *Did these stones and the sandstone rock help the victim facilitate his death?*

I moved closer. My eyes widened. *How did that get here?*

The sandstone boulder from Rosebud Bend had been the hangman's platform! *No one knew I kept the stone in my Jeep.*

I kicked the pile of river stones with the toe of my boot, uncovering a blood-crusted ring. I picked it up and wiped off the blood. My heart squeezed as I clasped the wedding band I had given Darrell.

A gentle wind rustled the leaves of the poplar. I spun around to see if anyone had followed me. That's when I glimpsed carvings in the tree's bark.

Here I hang,
With my face to the wall
And ...

Then I knew. My Darrell had hung from that tree.

A wave of disbelief and anguish swept over me. My knees buckled as I fell to the ground and pounded my fist into the sandstone rock. I wanted to kill the curse of the KGC and the Hackers with my bare hands.

I did not remember my return to the truck. I watched the sun hide behind the cover of mountains, leaving pitch-black darkness that matched the color of my soul. I had lost everything. Could *I* have caused it all? Did I also suffer the torment of the Hacker curse?

The afternoon replayed over and over in my mind. *Why did Darrell leave his truck in Magazine? How did he get to Race Horse Creek? How did he carry the sandstone to the top of the bluff? Two men would struggle with it over rough terrain. Besides, Darrell would never start the poem and not finish it. I knew he did not commit suicide. He died at the hands of the "others" just like Ezra. And, the wedding ring married my fate to his. I would be the next victim in this war of greed.*

My emotions exploded with alternate bursts of sorrow, remorse, and fear as I sat in Darrell's truck at the top of Sugar Loaf Mountain. Many hours passed before a surreal calmness washed over me. One task remained before I could leave the violence of these Ozark Hills. I resolved to end the curse of the Hackers and the KGC for good. Slamming into reverse, I turned the truck around and sped down the road. I knew what I had to do. I prayed Darrell would approve.

I drove to the *Gazette* and pulled into the alley with my lights off. I entered the back door and felt my way to my desk through the darkness. My hands trembled as I fired up the scanner on my computer. One at a time, I scanned the pieces of the map and emailed them to myself. After a quick exit, I headed to the Exxon station on the edge of town to buy a lighter.

The blackness of the night matched my mood as I pointed Darrell's truck toward Farm Road 273. An eternity seemed to pass before I pulled into Granny's drive. I jumped out of the truck and marched to the front porch, taking no pains to conceal my approach. Clutching the maps and lighter in hand, I ascended the wooden steps.

Granny's metal washtub would make a perfect funeral bier. I banged on the tub, summoning all within earshot to attend the ceremonial cremation of the cursed maps. Viva could not hear my drumbeat, but I felt certain the *friend* could not be far away. A disheveled Bessie and Granny appeared at the screen door with the tall silhouette of Buddy looming behind, barely visible in the darkness.

I flipped the tub upside down and crumbled the precious maps on the weathered platform. The dry, brittle paper burst into flames with a single touch of the lighter. Small tongues of fire leaped skyward as the maps turned to ash. I hoped the eyes of the rolling hills could see, and I would live free from their gaze forever.

No one made a move to stop me. Did they fear me, or did they think I had gone plumb crazy? I ran back to the truck and sped off into the night, pointing Darrell's truck toward Little Rock. Thoughts of being followed did not enter my mind. My value to either camp had burned with the flames. I would return to the university and, once again, immerse my life in academia, renouncing the sweet interlude with Darrell. Research and puzzles, which once filled the lonely corners of my life, would no longer be a part of me. A solitary email from Barber replaced them.

# Chapter XXI

Autumn had painted the trees with bright oranges, reds, and yellows. I bathed in the golden glow of a gentle fall sun as I sat on a bench at the far end of campus. My thoughts locked on the memory of Darrell and the meandering walks we took before the specter of Cowboy cast a long shadow on our lives.

*How could this have happened?*

I had come full circle from loneliness to a loving husband, and now, back to isolation. The melancholy afternoon provided no comfort to my aching soul. I feared to return to Barber for the funeral, and yet, the thought of Darrell being laid to rest without a final goodbye haunted me.

*Whose hand had taken the life of my beloved husband? Had I been the cause of it all?*

The half-finished poem carved in the poplar held the answer, but without Darrell, I would never know. I dabbed at the steady stream of tears as they trickled down my cheeks, fighting to hold in check a flood of emotions that would destroy me if I ever set them free. Solitude had been my constant companion, but hopelessness felt strange.

"You didn't attend my funeral."

Two large hands firmly caressed my shoulders, preventing me from turning to the source of the familiar masculine voice. I sat paralyzed.

"That's all right, Kay. I didn't go either," he whispered in my ear.

I shoved his hands away and spun around. I froze at the sight of the man in front of me.

I began pummeling his chest and crying. "I hate you. I hate you. I hate you."

The dam holding my emotions in check broke open wide, and I fell into Darrell's arms. He held me as I blubbered into his shirt like a heartbroken child. He shushed me over and over, his closeness a salve to my wounded soul. He stepped back and grasped my wet face in his hands.

"Listen, Kay, we need to get out of here. It's not safe."

I nodded, swiping at my runny nose with the back of my hand. We hoofed it to where he left his car. He drove straight to my motel room without asking for directions.

"Give me the key," he said.

I rummaged through my purse for the keycard. My swollen eyes made it hard to focus, but I finally wrapped my fingers around it.

He looked behind us and shoved me into the room before entering. Then he double-locked the doors.

"Are you okay?" Darrell asked.

My insides quivered, but I bobbed my head.

"I … I … I thought you were dead," I stammered.

"Then, my plan worked. I am sorry you got caught up in the charade, Kay."

A whirlwind of emotions churned inside me. Happiness, sorrow, fear, anger, and disbelief fought for first place. My gaze followed him as he moved about the room. I feared to blink in case Darrell disappeared like a wisp of smoke. *So, I'm not a widow*, I thought.

"Listen carefully. We don't have much time. Gather all your things and be ready to leave. Skeeter will be here in a few minutes with a pickup truck." Darrell inched the curtain to the side and scanned the parking lot.

I squeezed the bridge of my nose between my thumb and forefinger. I didn't understand how he ended up here. "What happened? Who hanged from that rope? Why is Skeeter coming here?"

Darrell heaved a sigh. Did he think I should just do as he ordered without asking?

"I'll tell you as much as I can, but when Skeeter arrives, we're gone."

I tossed my belongings in the suitcase.

"I left my truck in Magazine and took the bus to Memphis just like you did. I hoped you would come back with me, and we could undo all the chaos you had stirred up with the map. When I returned, Skeeter met me. It seemed when I followed you, I had given my *friend*, as you called him, clues to your whereabouts. We had to do something. He would have come after you."

Darrell paused and peeked out the window again. He scraped his hand through his hair.

"Skeeter pretended to be my *friend's* ally. They used to meet at the Pollyanna and make plans to steal the map. I never knew the old guy had it in him to carry that off … but he did."

So Skeeter played double agent with the man in the tan shirt and tie. I, too, marveled at his ability to trap a treasure hunter.

"They conjured up a plan to take me into the mountains and stage my suicide. I would hang myself, just like Grandpa Ezra."

Visions of poor Ezra hanging in the jail and the poem about Ora flashed before me. Ezra had failed to escape the others, but somehow Darrell had. The numbness of shock wore off, allowing dozens of questions to flood my mind.

"How did you get free? Skeeter's a big man."

"Kay, you're still rattled. Skeeter helped me. I switched clothes with my *friend* … his tan shirt and blue tie for my plaid shirt and jeans. We were similar in size, so it worked great. The treasure hunter swung from that rope. One less to worry about, though there will be more."

I slumped my shoulders. How many more treasure hunters existed?

"Will we always have to be on guard?" I asked.

"No, that's why I staged my hanging. I wanted us to be free of all this death and turmoil."

My husband had murdered a man, and I had no qualms with it. That surprised me, but I felt this overwhelming need to be together, to be safe.

"All of those people … the police and the undertaker. They could see the dead man was not you."

"They knew the plan. We buried my secret with the treasure hunter, and the sentinels will never tell. An army of sentinels guards these hills with a mighty force, Kay. You should know that by now."

*Oh, my gosh. Viva!* "What about your mother? She won't

survive if she thinks you are dead?"

"Mom knows. She went to Texas with Bessie after the funeral. We'll meet up with them at the Brazos. That's where all outlaws go to hide." He smiled at his weak attempt at humor.

"You sure threw a kink in my getaway." He chuckled. "Skeeter took me back to Magazine, and my truck was gone."

So, Darrell left his truck in Magazine for his escape, and I had ruined that. I ruined a lot of things. I prayed Darrell wanted me with him. He came to me. That must mean something.

"Pure genius to burn the maps." He clasped his hands behind his back and nodded. "Skeeter and I watched from the top of the mountain. That surely ended the insane search for the treasure."

My eyes widened. "You weren't mad? I burned the only map. How could you not be mad?" Men had lost their lives looking for the map, and I burned it. How could they not care?

"Skeeter knows where the treasure is. He doesn't need a map. Oh, and I know, but I am dead." His twisted humor grated on my frazzled nerves. "Only outsiders need a map to steal what belongs to the sentinels."

Darrell pulled the curtain back once again and glanced through the window. I noticed his barren ring finger.

"I have something for you if you still want it," I said.

I opened the side pocket of my purse and removed his wedding ring.

"Will you put this back on?"

I held my breath, hoping for a good answer.

He smiled and extended his hand. "Place it on my finger, Kay. This time I won't lose it."

I felt relief and a little niggling doubt as I slid the ring on his left hand. Viva, Bessie, Granny, and even Darrell had all tainted the truth with lies. I still trusted no one, but I must choose a life with him or return to the prison of loneliness. I chose the stranger I knew, my husband, the man I hoped would keep me safe.

Truly, this time, my life would begin anew. I had my husband, and soon I would have Viva and Bessie, too. I had never been fond of Viva, but I could tolerate her. She had a way of ignoring any truth that did not suit her. I would do the same. We could manage. However, I loved Bessie and the sultry Brazos Bottoms. I now had a family.

"Are you packed? Skeeter is here."

"All but my computer."

"Erase the disc. I don't want any trace of our old life hanging for someone to latch on to."

The request seemed strange to me, but I wanted to keep the peace.

As Darrell loaded my things in the pickup, I began to erase files. One by one, I deleted any information that pertained to the life I once had. The last file for deletion read *MAP*. I pressed the delete key, and a message appeared. Press "Yes" to continue or "Cancel." The cursor hovered over the "Yes" button.

"Kay, are you ready?" Darrell called from outside. "We need to get going."

"Just a minute."

I hesitated before sliding the cursor to "Cancel." I clicked the button and closed the lid.

# Chapter XXII

The tiny cabin did not meet my expectations. Darrell promised a quaint getaway, a honeymoon of sorts, a place to reconnect and sort out our future as well as our past. Instead, two shuttered windows on the face of a wooden box stared at me with hollow eyes.

"Kay," Darrell shouted.

I gasped, his voice dragging me away from my thoughts.

"Honey, we've got to keep moving, or we won't be in before dark."

The sun dipped low in the western sky, spilling shadows on the prairie floor. I did not want to be outside in the darkness. Picking up my small suitcase and computer, I resumed the uphill climb to the cabin. I twisted the knob and pushed, but the door did not budge. I lunged, slamming the door hard with my shoulder until the heavy wooden slab flew open. A quick perusal of the room revealed a small kitchen to the left facing a sofa that had seen better days on the right. Not what I expected.

I lugged my bundles to the bedroom at the back of the cabin and dropped them on the bed. A faint plume of dust swirled and sparkled in failing sunlight. I stared at the dancing dust beams as they settled, totally numbed by my surroundings.

"Honey, what on earth are you doing?"

Again, his voice jolted me. I snapped back to the moment, summoning a smile before I turned.

"Just trying to decide where to put everything."

My answer sounded ridiculous. One small suitcase and a computer did not require a lot of study.

He threw back his head and released a belly laugh.

"Tell you what, you figure out where to put *everything,* and I'll get the rest of our stuff," he said, grinning ear to ear. His tension since the first time I mentioned Cowboy had evaporated.

In no time at all, Darrell delivered the remaining boxes filled with food and cooking utensils then busied himself preparing our evening meal. The warm glow of two kerosene lamps filled the night with magic. Fried ham with pork and beans comprised our candlelight dinner for two. The man I married returned, replacing the stranger I had lived with for months. *Maybe, just maybe, we could find the happiness I dreamed of.*

Morning broke with buttery beams of sun streaming through the window. The fire in the potbelly stove had burned to ashes, offering no defense against the chilly autumn air. As I pulled the covers over my nose and snuggled deeper into the warm bed, I peered about the empty room. The cabin held its breath in silence, waiting for me to stir. The stillness overwhelmed me.

"Darrell?" I waited. "Darrell?" My voice louder this time,

I sat up, fully awake.

The magic of last night disappeared. He had left.

I shivered. Maybe from the cold or *maybe* Darrell's desertion. Either way, I had no choice but to slip on my house shoes and gather more wood.

The overgrown path challenged my flimsy slippers. I tip-toed, cursing myself every inch of the way. Twenty feet down the path, a muted, steady hissing sound teased my ears. I stopped to listen. Moments passed. *Nothing.* I took a few halting steps. Hissing again. Something protested my approach. Glancing down at my feet, I saw it. A dark coiled mass writhed as it vibrated its tail, barely discernable in the mottled blend of grass, rocks, and shadows. It pulled its upper torso into a tight S-shape and threw its head back to reveal a startling white interior.

My heart pounded in my chest, pulsing blood through my body. I froze. Screams lodged in my throat, silenced by hopelessness. No one would hear me.

Suddenly, a large branch shot over my shoulder and pinned the viper to the ground.

A black man loomed over the wriggling reptile. He kept one hand on the branch, securing the diamond-shaped head in place.

"Git me a twig. One with some bend to it," he ordered.

I mustered enough wits about me to do as he instructed. Brandishing the twig like a whip, he cracked the spine of the snake six inches below its darting tongue. All motion ceased. He had broken its back.

I dissolved into a convulsing blob of tears.

"You be fine now, ma'am."

His calm manner soothed me, but I could not stop

blubbering. Here I stood in my nightgown and robe sobbing uncontrollably. The stranger waited while I struggled to pull myself together.

"Who are you? What are you doing here?" I stammered. My rudeness, fueled by fear, did not phase the man.

"Name's Moses. Moses Trammel. Miss Bessie asked me to keep my eye on yo'. Sho' peers to be a good thing I did."

I could not agree more.

"Bessie sent you here?"

"Yep."

I glanced at the snake, motionless except for spasmodic flexes of the jaw. A snake can bite up to an hour after death. Darrell had told me this.

"What kind is he, Moses?"

"Cottonmouth. I ain't never seen one this far from the river. Sho'nuff dunno how he got here," he said, wagging his head back and forth.

I couldn't care less about how the snake got here. I only wanted to get back to the cabin. I turned and ran as fast as I could, leaping through the knee-high grass.

Safe inside the cabin, I turned, expecting to see Moses behind me. Instead, I saw him trudging down the hill.

"Wait! Come back," I said.

He paused and looked my way, but did not move. I waved my hands. I needed to talk to him. He shrugged and made his way up.

"Come in." I said it more like an order than a request, but he didn't seem to mind.

He removed his sweat-stained cap and stepped inside. I motioned him to sit at the table and prepared a fresh pot of coffee.

"So, Bessie asked you to keep an eye on me?"

"Yes' um."

"Why would she do that?"

His wince etched deep valleys in his forehead. He wrapped both hands around his cup and leaned forward.

"I best let yo' take that up with 'er."

We observed each other across the table. His smooth, coffee-colored face lacked expression, but his dark brown eyes burned holes right through me. He stood and walked toward the door.

"Don't leave me." He stopped. "Please."

"Not goin' anywhere, ma'am. Jus' clearing my head." He twisted his old cap as if to squeeze the truth out of it. He spoke slow and steady, like a man who did not relish what he had to say. "You sho' in a heap of trouble, ma'am," he said, kneading the cap into a wad. "That cottonmouth didn't get thar by himself. It kin kill with one strike ... but it's not the deadliest snake in these hills. Yo' is sitting in the shadow of sentinels, ma'am, and their enemies play fo' keeps. Somehow, someway yo' ended up with the only thing dey want ... the map."

Moses lifted his head and stared out the window.

"Dey squeezed yo' outta the herd and are circling ... jes waiting for the kill."

"But, I don't have the map," I squealed in protest.

"Don't talk to Moses like he a fool. Miss Bessie done tol' me all 'bout it."

"I burned it. The whole valley saw me burn it." I threw both my arms open wide.

"Dey saw yo' burn somethin'. But, it weren't no map."

If no one believed I burned the map, it served no purpose.

"Darrell knew I had both pieces of the map when he came to Memphis. Why didn't he take it then?"

"Miss Bessie say Darrell was scared to raise a ruckus. No, he had to get yo' by yur'self."

My mouth went dry. Moses' words rang true. I had been a willing fool.

*"Hackers weren't good enough for the KGC. Remember, they hung my grandpa, and I tried to steal their treasure. Even Ora didn't want her own grandson in the house, and Granny disowned her granddaughter because she married me."*

Darrell's words echoed in my head. His allegiance lay with the treasure, not with me.

The truth stung like the tail of a scorpion. Darrell and Viva had played well. I no longer existed to anyone but Darrell. He could do as he wished. The world on the other side of my window harbored evil beyond my control. I no longer wanted in. I had to trust Bessie and, by default, Moses.

He shifted back and forth on his feet. "Get yur things and come wit me, ma'am. Miss Bessie and me will hide yo'."

My eyes darted about the room, taking inventory of the remnants of my life. An isolated cabin, a computer with a treasure map, and a few belongings completed the paltry list. My world with Darrell lived only in my imagination.

"Yo' need to hurry if yo' is comin'," he urged. "I'll bring my ol' truck up here an' yo' jes be ready."

The ancient truck rattled up the road and came to an abrupt stop. I scrambled into the back of the pickup bed and pulled empty feed sacks about me. The ride punished and bruised my body as we jostled over rocks and ruts. My journey had just begun. It would be rough, but I felt free. The wind swirled about my face, lifting the lies Darrell and Viva told … the lies I told myself … and scattered them like dust in the blue Texas sky.

# Appendix

# Author's Notes

Often a writer conjures up a vision and weaves it into an intriguing tale. These, the truly gifted artists, pay homage to the mundane by transforming it into magic. On rare occasions, the story picks a writer, insisting they give shape and form to a tale beyond the scope of imagination. *Dust of Lies* is such a tale, born from conversations meant to pass the time. The topic, Jesse Cole James. The source, Jesse Cole's grandson. The life of this solitary figure known as Cowboy captivated me, and I badgered his grandson mercilessly over the years.

Jesse Cole James claimed to be the son of Jesse Woodson James and Emma Anders. He told the family he grew up in West, Texas, and Plainview, Texas. He attended the monkey rhyme school house with Joe Robales and had a redheaded sister named Mary. He said he spent time with his father in Texas before arriving in Arkansas. Before he married Ora, he warned her she and the family would always be in grave danger.

I asked his grandson what he made of these stories passed down through generations.

"This is what my grandpa told us. My dad and his family always lived in fear. I believed them. The problem is we have never been able to prove it. This tormented my dad all his life," he replied simply.

My curiosity rivals that of a cat. I researched Cowboy's life, combing ancestry sites and the internet, searching for threads to support his story. Finding meat on the bones of history challenged me. My biggest break in the puzzle came with the discovery of Plainview, Texas, in Houston County. Cowboy's riddles took on meaning. An elderly niece, related to Ora, provided many of the colorful stories that fleshed out the persona of the man.

The controversy surrounding Jesse James is alive and well. Many believe the traditional story that Jesse James died in St. Joe, Missouri, at the hands of Bob Ford. I do not. Many holes in the original story emerged with my research, and I continue to pursue these clues. However, the story of Cowboy does not revolve around the death date of Jesse James. Cowboy was conceived in the spring of 1881, long before the demise of the conventional Jesse.

The characters of Jesse Cole James, Ora Price, Ellie Townsend, and Ezra Hacker are based on real events and family lore. Sarah Vaughn Snow believed her father, Joe Vaughn, to be Frank James, brother of Jesse James. She co-authored a book titled *This Was Frank James* in 1969. Granny Snow, aside from the claim that her father was Frank James, is fictional. Ben Townsend, Willis Lang, James Hammett Anders, Ida Anders, Pauline Anders, and Martha Anders are all based on historical figures, but I strung their lives together with literary license to create a plausible narrative of the events surrounding Cowboy's life. Sweet Bessie, born mainly in my writer's mind, represents a real person I met but did not get to know due to her untimely death. Viva, Darrell, Buddy, Skeeter, and Moses Trammel are products of my imagination. Kay is harder to define. I wanted to take the reader with me on my journey to uncover the truth. Kay embodies my drive, curiosity, and background, but, for the record, I never stole a map.

The events of the story are artificially embedded into real towns and topography in the states of Arkansas and Texas and may or may not have a literal historical foundation.

I wrote *Dust of Lies* to memorialize the family stories, as well as to make sense of Cowboy's riddles. Mission accomplished on that front. To those who believe Jesse James's story ended in 1882, I hope you enjoy this book as a work of fiction. To those who do not believe history is always set in stone, I ask that you open your mind to the possibilities that Cowboy's story offers.

# Sources

Texas State Historical Association

Library of Congress, Manuscript Division,
    WPA Federal Writers' Project Collection

Handbook of Online Texas

Soldiersforgotten.com
    (Lang Letter)

Genealogy.com
    (Calamity Jane Letter to James O'Neil November 30, 1889)

# Acknowledgements

Writing a book is one of the hardest things I have ever done. It is difficult to string thousands of words together and hope they convey the story you desperately want to tell. I could not have done it without several special people who would not let me quit.

I am especially grateful to Jessie Cole's grandson who shared many of the details and stories found in the book. Family lore is a precious gift, and I appreciate he trusted me to do it justice.

Vivian Zabel played a key role in the completion of this story. I began writing in 2012, but put it aside to gather dust while I dealt with my daughter's illness. In 2017, I found the file on an old computer, and asked Vivian to read my manuscript. The time had come to mark it with a big black X or finish what I had started. Vivian told me to get busy and write the book. She stuck with me every step of the way.

A big thank you to my longtime friend, Suzanne Franz, who had me read the story to her over the phone because she could not wait to hear the next chapter. That's a good friend, folks.

I truly appreciate Cheyenne Olson, an old college friend, who provided feedback and encouragement on the plot. She is honest to a fault and did not let me get by with anything.

I am thankful for Brenda Irwin. She is the only person who read the book from cover to cover and encouraged me all the way. She is a reading specialist, as well as my boss's wife, so I couldn't fire her for a bad review.

On a personal note, I want to thank my brother, Stephen Davenport. He loved the book, but he loves everything I do. I needed someone who unconditionally adores me to erase the low points along the way.

On a professional note, I want to thank the crew of 4RV Publishing. Cheryl, my editor, put the shine on a rough manuscript. Rachel always stepped up to offer pointers. Joey C kicked my behind a few times to move me over hurdles. And, Vivian, as usual, kept a watchful eye on the whole process.

Most importantly, I credit my daughter. She attended the OWFI Conference with me where I won second place in my category. The next morning, she announced to her Sunday school class that her mother was writing a book. I could not let her tell a fib in church.

G.K Davenport, a first-time novelist, holds a degree in Chemistry from Oklahoma State University as well as a degree in accounting from Northwestern Oklahoma State University. She is currently employed as a Chief Financial Officer of an automotive dealership and resides with her family in northwest Oklahoma.

Next from G.K. Davenport:

next two books in the
— **Dust Chronicles** —
Dust & Redemption
Dust & Deliverance

CPSIA information can be obtained
at www.ICGtesting.com
Printed in the USA
BVHW041409200220
572913BV00009B/536